Tattycoram

Tattycoram

AUDREY THOMAS

GOOSE LANE

Edited by Laurel Boone.
Cover and interior design by Julie Scriver.
Cover image detailed from *The Bohemian* by Adolphe William Bouguereau,
courtesy of ARC – Art Renewal Center.
Printed in Canada by Friesens.
This book is printed on acid-free paper that is 100% recycled,
ancient-forest friendly (100% post-consumer recycled).
10 9 8 7 6 5 4 3 2 1

Library and Archives Canada Cataloguing in Publication

Thomas, Audrey, 1935-
Tattycoram / Audrey Thomas.

ISBN 0-86492-431-3

I. Title.

PS8539.H62T38 2005   C813'.54   C2005-900949-7

Published with the financial support of the Canada Council for the Arts,
the Government of Canada through the Book Publishing Industry
Development Program, and the New Brunswick Culture and Sports Secretariat.

Goose Lane Editions
469 King Street
Fredericton, New Brunswick
CANADA E3B 1E5
www.gooselane.com

To my dear neighbours,
Mick and G. English, who enjoy a good story

Question: What is your name?

Answer: N. or M.

Question: Who gave you this name?

— *The Book of Common Prayer*

Wash off my foul offence
And Cleanse me from my Sin
For I confess my Crime and see
How great my Guilt has been.

In Guilt each part was form'd
Of all this sinful Frame;
In Guilt I was conceived and born
The Heir of Sin and Shame.

> — *Psalms, Hymns and Anthems*
> *Used in the Chapel of the Hospital for*
> *the Maintenance and Education of*
> *Exposed and Deserted Young Children*
> (London, 1774)

Tattycoram

I

There is a small round spot on the top of my head where the hair will never grow. When I was young, I was sure this was where my mother's tears rained down in the days before she gave me up, her sadness soaking through to my skull. My foster mother told me I was eight weeks old when they put me in her waiting arms. Eight weeks of tears, wearing away that place on the top of my head like water wearing a hollow in a stone.

Years later Matron commented on it when they were washing our hair in preparation for cutting; she thought at first I had the ringworm.

We had to believe, you see, that our mothers wept, that they loved us dearly and hated to part with us, that they thought about us every day of their lives forever after.

We had been left at the hospital by our mothers, except for Agnes Lamb, who had been found under a bush in Mecklenburg Gardens. The fairies had left her there. The rest of us were handed over like a parcel, registered in the big book Mr. Brownlow kept locked in his desk: Girl, eight weeks, No. 19,176. Then washed, dressed in new clothes, christened in the chapel and given a new name. I was Harriet Coram.

Did I cry when the water touched my head? Did I think it was my mother's tears?

And then a long journey in a wagon, held close under the shawl of a woman who did not smell like my mother (who smelled spicy) as we bumped our way out of London. "Hush, hush," she said and put me to the breast, but I howled and turned away my head. "Ah," said the strange voice, "you'll suck when you're hungry enough."

"It was a long journey," my foster mother told me, "and you howled nearly the entire way. But you weren't the only one. Two dozen of you, swaddled like saveloys in penny buns, and most of you howling, poor little things. We stopped at an inn for refreshment. Some of the nurses made sugar-tits and dipped them in ale to make their babies sleepy, but I didn't want to do that. When we returned to the wagon, I lay down in the straw and tucked you in beside me and began to tell you about myself and your new father and grandfather and Sam and Jonnie and his little twin that died. Hannah, we had named her, and now she was buried in the churchyard with the others. When I thought of her I began to weep — the wound was still so fresh, you see. My breasts leaked, just thinking about her. The tears seemed to soothe you and you fell asleep for a bit. When you awoke, you took the breast so greedily I ached."

She smiled, remembering. "Little greedy guts, your father used to call you, whereas Jonnie . . . Jonnie would fall asleep. I had to tickle the soles of his feet to get him to continue. I sometimes wondered if he missed his twin, if there wasn't something in him that wanted to go to her. He was never very strong, unlike you. Do you think he is still alive?"

And now it was my turn to say "Hush, hush" and to comfort her, for she was dying and knew she would never see either of her sons again in this world.

Father had brought her a posy of spring flowers and laid it on her pillow.

"Lovely," she said, "lovely." And then she died. My real mother — the only mother I had ever known.

Sam was our big brother. He was nine years old when I arrived in Shere; after him came the dead babies in the churchyard, then finally the twins, Hannah and Jonathan, but Hannah died as well. Each baby had a little lamb carved by Grandfather, a whole flock of little lambs side by side in the green grass. If Hannah had not died, I wouldn't be there, safe and loved, with Father and Mother and Sam and Jonnie and Grandfather, who had been blind since he had the smallpox at the age of six.

(Do I really remember a large, rough hand moving gently over my face the night I arrived, a hand rough as a cat's tongue, making my acquaintance through the tips of his fingers?)

Grandfather had a gift: he could carve anything. The little outbuilding where he worked smelled sweetly of fresh shavings. He had carved the rood screen for our church — all wild roses, eglantine, wood anemone and the wildflowers which grew all around. It was the talk of the county, and people came from far and wide to see it. Sam told me he had once asked Grandfather how he could carve flowers and birds when he couldn't see. "And he said, 'I wasn't always blind, Samuel. I had six years of looking and I was a country lad. I liked getting up close to things even then. What a child sees in the first six years of his life, he never forgets. It's in there, somewhere, and all he has to do is draw it out.'"

Grandmother was dead, and our other grandparents as well, but Grandfather was enough. As I grew, I liked to sit beside him on his bench while he worked. Newel posts for one of the big houses or graveboards or toys for the wealthy children in the neighbourhood or his big project — misericordes for the cathedral at Guildford.

It was Grandfather's gift, Sam told me many years later, which set us apart from the other labourers' families, that even provided us with little luxuries. Times were bad and Father's wages were very low, but with Grandfather's carving and Mother's needlework and the money from the hospital, we managed. I was too young to understand how the workhouse loomed as a threat over village life. No one ever wanted to end up there, but some couldn't help themselves. We managed quite well. Always wheaten bread, not the rough barley loaves. Real tea, and once a week a nice piece of bacon. I think I took it for granted that everybody could live like that if they wanted to.

Sam worked at haying and harvesting, along with Mother and Father, while Grandfather kept an eye on us. (That was his joke.) And soon enough we were put to work as well, as bird-scarers in the fields. Grandfather made us each a clapper; Sam took us out and set us down wherever we were needed. We liked making noise, whirling the clappers around and shouting, "Bad birds, bad birds." We got a penny a day between us and proudly gave it to Mam, who told us she didn't know how she'd manage without us, not yet four and already bringing in wages!

Grandfather made me a doll with a wooden head and arms and Mother made her a body stuffed with bits of rag. She had a blue checked dress sewn from a gypsy handkerchief, and I loved her to distraction. Jonnie had a wonderful wooden chicken on wheels with a hollow on its back where a wooden egg fitted.

The egg went round when he pulled the hen along by a string.

Sam knocked down a boy who said I was a bastard. Father said, "Show him to me, and I'll knock him down again."

"What's a bastard?" I asked.

We all slept upstairs in the same room except for Grandfather, who preferred to sleep in his workshop. Each night he would rise from his chair and wish us all a goodnight and a God bless. He never needed a lantern, for his feet knew the way, how many steps to the door, how many to round the corner of the cottage, how many to his own door.

He shaved himself with a wicked razor, and once a month Mother sat him down outside and cut his hair, then Father's, then Sam's, then Jonnie's. "As for you," she said to me, "you and your bird's nest." My hair was always in a curly tangle and I cried when she combed it out. "I should cut it, I suppose, but I can't bear to," winding one of my curls around her finger.

The children in the village loved Grandfather because, at Christmas and birthdays, he gave them wooden whistles or little wooden spinning tops. Once, for a crippled boy, a complete Noah's Ark. His mother came, weeping, to thank him. We asked him why we couldn't have a Noah's Ark as well, and he told us we could roam around and see real animals any day of the week.

"But not the 'potamus, Grandfather," Jonnie said, "not the 'potamus and not the giraffe."

"I'll tell you what," said Grandfather, "I'll make you each a throne." Which he did.

When he had time, Sam took us on adventures. Sometimes we went as far as the gypsy camps in the Hurtwood. The gypsy children were dirty and made faces, but I liked the women in their flouncy skirts and gold earrings. They gave us tea in tin mugs, and I can still remember the way the tea tasted of the heather, a brown, slightly bitter taste.

They lived in tents and the men stole horses — or that's what people said in the villages. The women could put a curse on you, so if they offered you something for sale, the village women said, you'd better buy it or your milk might dry up or a horse might kick you in the head. Mother said she had never heard the women cursing anybody, but Father laughed and said, "Then why do you buy from them?"

We liked the gypsies, and we liked the way Sam took us on adventures and lifted us over stiles if we couldn't manage on our own.

Sam and Jonnie were fair and had lovely reddish hair like Mother. In the sun it shone like new pennies. Father was fair as well and Grandfather was grey. I was the only one whose hair was dark, and that was because I had another mother long ago who couldn't take care of me.

"Why couldn't she?"

"She just couldn't."

"Why?"

We went to church on Sunday mornings, everybody except Father, who said it was his day of rest. Most of the fathers didn't go. What I liked best about church was the pump organ that ground out the hymns and the graveyard where the tall, thin stones and boards tilted every which way. Some of them were so old and weathered the names had disappeared. The dead slept all together, under a soft green blanket, until Resurrection Day, when everybody would jump up and begin dancing. It would be just like Harvest Festival. Even the dead babies would jump up and clap their little hands. I liked the idea of the babies dancing, especially little Hannah, for whom I had a particular affection.

Jonnie and I went with Mother and the other women and children to gather rushes for the rushlights and laid them out, just so, for dipping. We gathered mushrooms and hazelnuts and, best of all, we picked the hurts when they were ripe. Oh, the hurts were lovely, and we quickly filled Mother's basket and then our own. We ate almost as many as we picked and came home with blue lips and blue tongues, Mother as well. There was nothing so good as a bowl of hurts, with a bit of milk if you could get it, hurt preserves if you had any sugar to spare.

It must have rained during my early years in the village — I know it did, for I can remember the sound of the rain on the thatch, as Jonnie and I lay in our little truckle bed upstairs; but when I look back like this, it is as though my childhood, from the time I was put into my real mother's arms until the day I left at the age of five and a half, my childhood was like some seamless garment which covered me lightly and kept me from all harm. I think if I hadn't had that I might have turned out quite a different person. Like poor Elisabeth Avis, perhaps.

A stream ran through the village, the Tillingbourne, very clear, shallow and fast-flowing. Sometimes Sam tied us both to a rope and the rope to one of the old trees, which leaned so far over the water they almost met their reflections. We were to sit there and be good while he went off somewhere with his friends. We did not like to be tied up, but Sam's knots were firm and we were stuck. We must not tell Mother; we must solemnly swear, and we solemnly did. I suppose we were about three years old at this time, so Sam would be twelve.

That was how we were the first to see the princess come

floating by. She had on a long white dress and was looking at something in the water so we couldn't see her face, just her hair, which was yellow, like wheat, her long hair streaming down her back.

We called to her to come and untie us, but she paid no attention and disappeared towards the bridge.

"A princess," I said to Jonnie, and he nodded. How we wanted to get up and follow her, but the rope kept us prisoner upstream.

And then, after a while, we heard the women in the village crying out to her and greeting her, and we were cross with Sam because it was his fault we were missing all the excitement. No doubt at that very moment they were handing her the golden crown.

And then Mother's voice, frantic, calling, "Sam! Sam! Sam! Sam!" but of course he was far away and we had made a solemn promise not to tell.

She found us anyway and Sam got a beating when he came home. He told me later that he too was frantic when he arrived at the spot where he had left us and all that was there was the rope, still tied to the tree.

"I saw a princess," I told Mother. But it wasn't, only a girl from one of the big houses over towards Gomshall, and nobody knew how she had fallen in or why she couldn't get up, a big girl like that. And so we learned a new word: drowned. The whole village went to the funeral at Gomshall — all the villages went — everybody wearing white, not black, because she was so young.

Mother hugged us until we hurt. For a long time we were not allowed to float our twig boats in the stream, standing on one side of the bridge and leaning over, then rushing to the other side to see whose boat came through first.

There was something called an inquest.

At Christmastime the rector's wife and the Misses Bray gave a party for all the children. That's when we got new clothes. What we liked best were the sweeties and the oranges, although oranges made me cry. I couldn't say why; I don't know why. The rector's wife said, "Well, who's an ungrateful child?" The moon had turned to ice and the ruts in the road were frozen. We sat close to the fire on our thrones while Grandfather told us stories. The bells rang in the New Year; we were allowed a sip of blackberry cordial before we went up to bed. Sam stayed up later now that he was nearly grown. Mother told us to go straight to sleep and never to look at the moon through glass.

And there was a lady, long ago, who was walled up in the church. All she had were two little places where she could look out and be handed food. She must have been very bad. I asked my mother, "What did she do?"

"She was a holy woman."

"What's a holy woman?"

"Someone good, someone who wants to be alone and think about God."

"But why did she have to be shut up to do that?"

"I don't know. There are other stories."

"Tell me the other stories."

"You're too young."

"I am five."

"Yes, I know that," and her face went sad.

I asked Grandfather.

"Grandfather, do you know any stories about the lady who was walled up in the church?"

"None fit for your ears," he said, and would say no more.

Sam and Father worked every day in the fields. They got up before daybreak and came home at dusk. Our big brother had little time for us now. On Sundays he went roaming with his friends. Sometimes at night, if he came up and we were still awake, he made us shadow puppets on the walls, but mostly he just smiled at us in passing and patted our heads. We were old enough to scare off the birds by ourselves. We drove the small birds away from the turnip seeds and the rooks away from the peas. The rooks mocked us but the sparrows flew away from our clappers. "Away away, you black devils, away away! You eat too much, you drink too much, you carry too much away."

When Grandfather worked at his carving, he would sometimes pause and touch my cheek. It was as though there were tiny hairs on the ends of his fingers, like the hairs on the bumblebee, collecting something from me that he might want for later use. I noticed he did not do this to Jonnie, but Jonnie was a boy and boys were not overfond of being touched.

Mother did mending and some fancy work for the Misses Bray. One day, she scrubbed us hard with yellow soap and took us with her. We saw a barn cat crossing the yard with a kitten in her mouth.

"It doesn't hurt them," Miss Louisa said. "The skin is very loose there, where she holds them."

"Why is she moving them?"

"Oh, something has bothered her, she's decided they would be safer under the house."

The kittens wore patches of brown and black and white; their eyes weren't open yet.

"Could we have one, Mammy? Could we have a little kitten?"

"They are too young to leave their mother," Miss Amelia said.

"But when they are not too young? Could we have one then?"

I looked up earnestly from where my brother and I were squatting to admire the kittens not yet moved. I caught my mother and the two sisters exchanging glances.

"Please, Mammy. I'll take good care and Jonnie will help me."

"We'll see."

We said our goodbyes and walked away towards home, swinging our arms, my mother unusually silent, for she often sang when she was out on a walk with us.

That evening, after tea, they sat me down in my little chair, my throne.

"Hattie," my mother said, "we have never made a secret of the fact that you are on loan to us from the good people at the hospital. We have loved you as our own little daughter and watched you grow. But now the time is coming when we must give you back." Her voice broke and she sobbed into her apron.

"Why?" I said, frightened, looking from one to the other. Father shook his head and said nothing, Sam sat silent, but Grandfather lifted me up and set me on his knee.

"That's the rules, Hattie. You would have gone last year except you had the scarlatina, and the Governors waited to be sure you were fit again, wanted to give you some extra months here in the country before you were removed."

"And will Jonnie go too?"

"No, Jonnie will stay here."

"Why, why will Jonnie stay? I've been a good girl, I've been as good as Jonnie."

"The rule doesn't apply to Jonnie, love, only to you."

"Why only to me?"

"Because you were lent us, from the Foundling, but Jonnie — Jonnie comes from here."

I slid down off Grandfather's knee.

"I won't go! I don't want to go!" I ran to my mother and pulled the apron from her face.

"Mam, don't make me go. I'll be gooder . . . I'll help. Don't make me go!"

"I can't change the rules, Hattie. I wish I could."

"Is that why I can't have a kitten? I won't be here when they're old enough?"

She nodded.

"Perhaps," said Grandfather, but without much conviction, "there will be kittens at the Foundling."

I struck out, in my terror and helplessness, at the very people who loved me. I could not understand why they couldn't help me. I picked up Baby and threw her at Jonnie, who was allowed to stay. The doll hit him smack in the middle of the forehead and he began to cry. Good.

"I hate you all," I cried, and rushed out the door, sobbing bitterly. Grandfather soon caught up with me. He took my hand and said nothing, just stood beside me until the worst of the storm had passed. Then he bent down, told me to climb onto his shoulders, and carried me home. Mother bathed my face with cool cloths, then took me up to bed. She brought Jonnie up; he had a lump on his head like his wooden egg.

"Hattie, tell your brother you are sorry for what you did."

"I'm sorry," I mumbled, but in my heart I wasn't — not even when he put his arms around me and cried that if I had to go he wanted to go too.

"You can't," I said, turning away from him. "It's the rules."

Only later did I understand that Jonnie stayed because he wasn't one of us, one of the Children of Shame.

The night before I left was a night of shooting stars. I was allowed to stay up — "She'll sleep on the way to London" — so Grandfather and I sat on the bench outside the cottage and waited.

"Hist!" he said. "There's one now."

And there it was, streaking across the sky.

"How can you tell, Grandfather, when you can't see them?"

"I don't know. Something changes."

"But they are so far away!"

"I can't explain it, I just know."

Soon there were dozens of them, flashing this way and that; my head was on a swivel, trying to catch them all. Mother came out and put a big shawl across our shoulders; it was cool, now, at night.

"What will they think if I send you back with the sniffles?"

From out in the wood an owl hooted — whoo whoo — and Grandfather said at last that it was time to go in.

"Remember this, Hattie," he said. "Wherever we are, we are all under the same sky."

As I lay in bed, too sad to sleep and cross that the whole family wasn't lying awake as I was, the smell of Grandfather's tobacco came through the open window; I knew that he was still there, sitting in the dark and listening to the mad dance of the stars up above.

2

The wagon came from Farnham and stopped in the square. I was dressed in my clean frock and a pair of shoes; my number was hung around my neck. I had to leave Baby behind — we were to bring no toys — but the Misses Bray had sent down a handkerchief baby, very tiny, with a face no bigger than a shoe button. Mother told me to tuck it in my pocket and perhaps Matron wouldn't notice. Father and Sam were off in the fields; they said their goodbyes at an early breakfast, and I stood at the door and watched them walk away, become smaller and smaller and then disappear. Jonnie was to walk down with Grandfather, Mother and me, but at the last minute he ran back inside and refused to come out. Mother was anxious that we not be late — she was coming with me — so she said we must leave him be and hurried me away.

The children from Farnham were already in the wagon, along with another foster mother.

"Climb up, climb up," said the driver, as he let down some steps. I clung to Grandfather even after Mother was seated and holding out her hands.

"You must go now, pet. There's a good girl." He lifted me up and my mother caught me.

Most of the children were crying and sobbing and I began to

cry as well, even though Mother was there beside me in her Sunday bonnet and shawl. She told me later that old Mrs. Shute, who was no longer right in the head, had heard the noise from her cottage nearby and come running out, convinced it was Judgement Day; she wanted to jump on and be taken to the place where the Lord would judge the quick and the dead. "'Tis the wailing wagon, 'tis the wailing wagon. Wait, wait for me!"

Small boys, not yet gone to the fields, ran after us shouting and throwing stones, and indeed we must have seemed comical, even grotesque, a great wagon full of children crying as though their hearts would break. A strange harvest, fruit of our fallen mothers' wombs, about to be delivered to the metropolis like a load of apples or melons.

More children climbed aboard in Dorking and in Guildford, where we stopped for bread and ale. Then, in the early afternoon, the sky darkened, streaks of lightning shot from it and thunder, which made us cry out in fear, and then a torrential downpour, as though even God were saying, "Don't do this. Turn back, turn back." We were not very wet, for the wagon had a tilt, but the sound of the rain and the early darkness just added to our misery. One of the horses slid and stumbled in the muddy highway, and for a terrifying moment it seemed as if we might all be pitched out onto the road. The driver shouted and cursed and laid about with his whip, and then we were all right again.

There were other wailing wagons on the road that day but I didn't know it then. Small boys and girls, all frightened, all headed for the same place — cartloads of little bastards.

The great roar of London began even before we crossed the river, and now we were just one vehicle among many as we moved through the clogged streets towards Bloomsbury. The rain had stopped, but the air did not smell fresh, the way it did in the country after a rainstorm. It smelled of coal fires and decay and dung, a smell I would never get used to. But soon enough, the great iron gates swung open and our wagon rolled inside. The tilt was pulled back, my mother and the other women were helped down, and then we were lifted away and brushed clean of straw. Matron and her assistants were there to greet us. I clung to my mother, and they had to pry me loose while I screamed, "Mam, Mam, I'll be good, I promise," which set the others to crying as well. "Ma, Maa, Maaa," we bleated as we were led away, washed and fed, dressed in long muslin nightgowns and put to bed early in our little iron cots, the girls in one wing, the boys in another. Tomorrow, Matron said, would be soon enough for uniforms.

I had never slept alone in a bed before, and my small cot seemed enormous and cold too without Jonnie's warmth next to mine; no one had kissed me goodnight or told me they loved me. Even my handkerchief baby had been found and taken away from me. I twisted up a corner of the pillowcase to make another baby and sobbed myself to sleep. They could not really have loved me — Father, Mother, Grandfather, Sam, Jonnie — or they would not have cast me off like this. That was the terrible thing; they hadn't cared enough to rescue me.

"Will I ever see you again?" I had asked my mother, and she, her eyes red-rimmed from weeping, said, "Of course, I promise you. We shall come to visit on your birthday, and when you learn to read and write, perhaps you will write us letters."

"But who will read them to you?"

"The rector or his wife. One of the Misses Bray. Don't you worry about that."

But I no longer believed her — or not on that dark night. I knew I would never see any of them again. My mother could cry all she liked; she'd soon forget me.

Years later, when Sam told me about his first days on the convict ship, I thought, yes, I might just as well have been condemned to transportation for the wretchedness I felt that night and for many nights to come. Cut off from the family I loved, the landscape I loved, and the freedom I had enjoyed in our little village, I might just as well have been confined to prison. At least poor Sam knew what his crime had been; I did not yet understand mine.

Nurse slept at the end of the ward, behind heavy curtains. Once she started snoring, we could whisper, and we soon discovered that our beds were just close enough together that we could reach out and hold hands. That was how we often comforted ourselves at night, with whispers and a hand to hold, for when the moon was bright, its flickering light came through the barred windows and cast dreadful shadows on the walls. A chain of little girls in rough muslin nightgowns, holding hands, up one side of the ward and down the other, until one by one the hands dropped away, and we fell asleep.

The wet-beds didn't hold hands. They slept in special canvas cots right at the very end. They stayed there until they learned their lesson.

My new life at the hospital bore so little relation to the life I had led in the country — I was going on for six when I arrived — it was as though I had to start all over again. To begin with, there was the uniform, made of a heavy brown material which scratched our necks raw. On top of that was our apron and bib, and on our heads a strange tall, frilled cap. Almost as bad as the scratchy dress were the high laced shoes. Our feet were not used to shoes and they dragged us down. Just lacing them up to Nurse's satisfaction made us weep with frustration. Nurse scolded us: "You don't know how lucky you are." I soon taught myself never to cry in front of any of them, no matter what happened, no matter what the punishment. By the time I was eleven, I was known as "iron hands."

In the spring and summer we arose at six (five when we grew older), washed and dressed ourselves and were marched down to breakfast. In autumn and winter we could stay in bed until seven. Breakfast was always milk pottage or water gruel; dinner at noon depended on the day. Three times a week we had butcher meat, either beef or mutton; three times a week, for supper, we had bread and cheese. We never had fish or poultry, nor an egg, except on Good Friday or if our foster parents brought some on their annual visit. Mondays were always meatless. The food was adequate, more meat, in fact, than any of us were used to, but food does not taste the same when you are marched down to a dining hall to eat it, when a rap on the table tells you when to sit, another rap tells you when to begin, and you eat in silence. All our natural high spirits were pushed down by the countless rules and regulations. We never raised our voices; we girls never ran. Spontaneous gestures of any kind — a shout, loud laughter, an inappropriate giggle — usually led to reprimand and often to punishment. It was made clear to us, right from the beginning, that we were not like other children; our previous life in the country had been necessary for our bodily health, but that life was over now, just a brief interlude in a life that was to consist of service of one kind or another.

Although we would learn to read and write and cypher, we were not, because of this, to think ourselves above our station, which was low, very low indeed. The lowest.

For me, Sundays were both the best days and the worst. On Sundays we had chapel and the delight of singing in the choir, but on Sundays the ladies also came to visit. I can hear them still, their skirts going swish, swish, swish, as they moved around the dining hall, examining the dear little foundlings at their Sunday dinner. Swish, swish — and many with pretty children. We were as exotic to them as baby animals at a zoo.

"And do you enjoy your dinner, dear?"

"Yes, ma'am."

Stand up when spoken to and do not scrape your chair! Remember always who you are and how lucky you are to be here, for weren't you saved from the workhouse, a fate worse than death, or even death itself?

(Sometimes I lay on my back in the playground, risking punishment for grass stains on my clothes, just to see the sky and the free-ranging clouds.)

"Mama, why do all the children dress alike?"

"Because it's their uniform, darling."

"But Mama, do they wear it every day?"

"Of course."

"But why is it so ugly? Wouldn't they rather wear a pretty frock like mine?"

"I should think they are grateful to have anything to wear at all."

"But Mama —"

"Come along now, that's enough questions."

Every plate and mug had a picture of a lamb on it, a lamb with a sprig of thyme in its mouth. He shall feed his flock.

We went for walks with Nurse in the fields at the back of the hospital, but we girls were never allowed outside the gates. The servants gave us snippets of news from time to time, especially the cooks and the kitchen maids. We discovered that London was a big city full of lovely things to see and do: Punch and Judy shows and organ grinders with their monkeys, pie men and muffin men and halfpenny ices in the summer. Pleasure gardens and big parks right in the middle of the city. Once Cook had even seen the moon, close up, through a long glass. All life seemed to lie just outside the gates. We heard horses' hooves and distant laughter and, often, the urgent bells of fire engines as they hurried to a fire. London — the rest of London — was like fragments of a dream.

Mother came on my birthday, as promised, with kisses and hugs from all and a packet of hoarhound drops I was to share if Nurse approved. Jonnie had turned six the month before and was a big help to all. When he reached ten, he was to be apprenticed to the blacksmith and, eventually, would become a farrier.

"Mammy," I said, "I don't like it here. You must take me home."

She turned her face away and squeezed my hand.

"Is there another girl, now, Mammy, sitting on my throne?"

"Oh no, lovey, you were the last little girl. Your chair has been put away in Grandfather's shop, and Baby is wrapped up and put away as well."

"For when I come home?"

"For when you are all grown up and perhaps have little ones of your own."

And then our time was up.

She did not come on my seventh birthday, although I looked

out for her all afternoon. I did not know it, but Sam had been caught poaching, with his leg stuck in a mantrap. Jonnie had been with him, but Jonnie got away and ran off God knows where. Sam was locked up in one of the hulks, his foot all torn and twisted. There had been a trial and he was to be transported.

"Father suspected," Sam told me later, "and Grandfather knew in the way he always knew everything. They warned me more than once, but at first it was only hares we went after, and surely rabbits and hares belonged to all of us, like the birds of the air, not just to those in the big houses. Times were hard at home, and even with Grandfather's carving and Mam's bits of sewing and Father and me working from dawn till dark, there were days when it was kettle broth and barley loaves. We were saving for Jonnie's apprenticeship, a few coppers at a time. There were many men on the tramp, whole families even, as wages fell lower and lower. And I confess I liked the excitement. You had to be quick if you wanted to get away with poaching. The gamekeepers were pretty swift — and they had guns as well. Each side tried to outsmart the other.

"The first time I brought home a hare, Mam would have nothing to do with it. She dug a deep hole and buried it and put a pile of stones on top. It made me wild to see her taking less and less of her share of the dinner, making excuses.

"She could have fostered more children, using a bottle and spoon — they called it 'the metal mother,' she told me — but Father wouldn't let her, she suffered so when you left. It was like a game, really, the poaching. If she wouldn't accept what I snared, then I would sell it. There was a man in Gomshall who would buy anything, flesh or fowl, for the London market, no questions asked. I began a little store of coppers of my own, and

I bought a gun. And gradually I got bolder and went after game birds. The birds were my undoing, and taking Jonnie with me when I knew better. He begged and wheedled until I said all right, just this once.

"Just this once!

"When the trap bit down into my ankle, I let out a great howl, I couldn't help it, it hurt so much — the worst pain I had ever felt. I could hear the bones break.

"'Run,' I called to Jonnie, 'run for your life!'

"I thought he would run home, but he must have believed nothing could save him if he went back to the village, so he just disappeared. Seven years old and on the run and all because of me.

"I was taken to the infirmary at Guildford, and when they had done what they could for my foot, I had to stand trial at the assizes. They came to see me — Mother, Father, Grandfather — before I was led away. There was no news of Jonnie. He had vanished.

"The magistrate said he was going to make an example of me, never mind it was my first offence, never mind I had already been punished with a nearly useless foot. Transportation for fourteen years. Bang. All rise.

"Father went all the way to London to look for Jonnie, but no matter who he asked or where he asked, no one could help. Seven years old!" Sam drew his sleeve across his eyes. "Even now it makes me weep. And how Mother must have suffered. All her children gone now, me to Australia and you to the Foundling and Jonnie to God knows where."

"She lived in hope of seeing both of you again before she died."

"I wrote letters."

"She got only one, the first year you were out there. The rector came and read it out to them."

"I wrote more than one letter."

"They didn't arrive."

"Jonnie never found a way to send them a message?"

"Never. I think at first he was afraid. When he disappeared, everyone knew he must have been with you that night. Some thought at first our parents were hiding him. Tongues wagged. He said he once came back as far as London Lane, but he was frightened by some dogs and never tried again."

"He could have found a way to send word."

"Yes, I suppose so."

"You never asked him why not?"

"They were dead by that time — all those who loved him. Except me."

We sat quietly, thinking about the past, about what might have been. How resentful I had been when she didn't appear on my birthday! It was Mr. Brownlow who called me down and told me what had happened. Mother had asked the rector to send him word.

Now, surely, they would let me go home?

One night I awoke to a snick, snick, near my ear. I cried out but Nurse put her hand over my mouth. "Hush, you'll wake the lot of them. Go back to sleep." She had cut off a lock of my hair.

The other girls thought it was so romantic; it was obvious my real mother wanted a memento.

"Or maybe Nurse is a witch," Amy said, "and she wants to cast a spell on you."

"What sort of a spell?"

"I don't know what sort of a spell. We'll have to wait and see."

But nothing happened and she never did it again.

3

"If my mother ever came to claim me," said Caroline Bragg, "I'd spit in her eye."

We were in sewing class, making nightgowns for the babies and learning to hem sheets. The sewing mistress often left us alone; we were big girls now.

"I'd show her my back," said Amy Turtle, biting off a thread with her sharp little teeth.

"If she was a grand lady," Phoebe Sparrow said, "I'd go with her gladly."

Phoebe had good bones. She was sure her mother was an Honourable, if not a full-blown duchess. She had been seduced by the handsome gardener.

"What if he were handsome beyond belief? What if he handed her a pure white rose each morning as she walked the garden paths with her little lapdog in her arms?"

"What if the little dog bit him?" Amy said, and we all laughed together.

"Look at Mr. Twigg," she said, and his name set us to giggling. "Can you imagine our Mr. Twigg with an Honourable?"

"They can't all be as old as Mr. Twigg."

"Or as ugly!"

But there had been a girl and an under-gardener, right here

at the hospital, not so long ago. We were never to talk to any man except the Governors or the masters. Never. Cook said the girl had had a child who was found dead in the potting shed. Cook had been here for ages and had bristles growing out of her chin. She was not supposed to tell us things like that; we solemnly promised never to repeat them.

We had all lived in the country, had seen cocks mount hens, had seen dogs and even horses, but we had only a vague idea of what the gardener had done. Caroline said if you kissed a man six times, that would do it, but Caroline was a fool.

One day, when I was folding linen with Matron, I asked her about the mothers.

"Do the mothers ever come back to claim their children?"

She looked at me over her half-spectacles. Matron had a harsh manner when we were all together, but I had discovered she could be pleasant when alone with one or two.

"Why do you ask?"

"We . . . I was just wondering."

She put down her pen; she was marking the new sheets with waterproof ink, according to the ward for which they were destined.

"There have been cases — a few. A very few. If she marries a good man who is willing to take on another man's by — another man's child, then perhaps."

"Are the children asked? We heard that the children are asked."

"Asked what, Harriet?"

"Asked if they want to go."

"They are. I believe most of them say yes. But I remember a young lad a few years ago who chose to say no. He was in the band and wanted to join an army band when he was old enough. It was to his advantage to stay where he was, but his was a special case."

I thought about that mother. Settled with a kind and decent man, she tells him her story. Perhaps there were already other children, perhaps not.

"Well," says her husband, "we must be off to get him at once!"

They send a letter to Mr. Brownlow, Secretary, The Foundling Hospital, London: they will arrive on such and such a day to claim No. 825, a boy, and will bring the certificate with them. (No. 825 is now called Jeremiah Brown.)

When they arrive, Jem, who has been learning to play the cornet, is called out of his lessons and taken to the court room. Mr. Brownlow is there with Matron, one of the Governors, and a strange man and lady.

"Jem," says the lady, stretching out her arms, "dear John, I am your mother."

Jem looks down at his boots and says nothing.

"Jeremiah," says the Secretary, "this lady is your mother and she has come to take you home. How do you feel about that, my boy?"

And Jem says to the carpet, "I do not wish to be reclaimed, sir, I wish to remain here."

The mother's heart has been struck with a hammer. Her boy, her first-born child! He does not wish . . .

Mr. Brownlow, whom everybody knows was once a foundling himself — he makes no secret of it and we love him for this — says gently, "Is there any particular reason for this? Would you like time to think it over?"

Jem shakes his head; he will not look up. He thinks of his golden cornet; he thinks of marching in an army band.

"Jem," says his mother, "look at me, dear. Look at your poor mother who has always loved you." The paintings in their gilt frames mock her: *Pharaoh's Daughter Finding the Infant Moses*; *Christ Blessing the Little Children* . . .

At this cry, Jeremiah Brown raises his head and gives her such a look that she faints dead away.

Even this kindles no compassion in his heart; he does not know these strangers. In two years he will be old enough to join the army.

"May I go now, sir?"

And he leaves without a backward glance.

The Secretary turns to the stricken couple. Matron's smelling salts have brought the woman round, and she is quietly sobbing.

Mr. Brownlow shakes his head. "I'm sorry."

"Perhaps," says the stepfather, twisting his hat round and round, "he will change his mind? Perhaps the shock was too much for him, finding his mother after all these years."

"No. I don't think he will change his mind."

"Oh God," cries the mother, "could you call him back? Could I see him just one more time?"

But that is against the rules. The kind husband thanks the Secretary and leads away the weeping woman.

Could I do that? If my first mother came to reclaim me? Once I had seen her and satisfied my curiosity on that score? What name had she given me, before I became No. 19,176, Harriet Coram? Perhaps she simply called me Baby.

"Harriet," said Matron, "you are daydreaming again. You may go back to the sewing room — unless you have any more questions."

"No, Matron, thank you."

(But I did have one. The children who were claimed, were they happy? A ridiculous question and I knew better than to ask it. We were not brought up to think of happiness; we were to concentrate on Obedience and Duty.)

On Founder's Day, in October, we were given roast beef and plum pudding for dinner, and on Christmas Day we had the same, as well as an orange and a new penny under every cup. I had ten pennies tied in my handkerchief when I left the hospital, for what was there to spend them on?

We received new clothes once a year, before the May meeting of the Governors. As we grew we exchanged one ugly brown uniform for another.

There was some real happiness for me, however, within those stern walls, for I sang in the choir, and music was the one great blessing at the Foundling. Music on Sunday mornings helped me to endure Sunday dinner and being gawked at by the fashionable ladies. I would slip an anthem into my head and shut out the rest of the world.

Our choirmaster had been at the hospital for years — a fat, rosy man who I later thought looked more like a publican than a man who had dedicated his life to music. But it was music he loved, music he was passionate about, and, unlike the rest of our teachers — who seemed to suffer collectively from a lack of imagination, and hence imparted nothing to us of the magic of numbers or the pleasures of reading; who, I sometimes suspected, could barely read and write above the infant level themselves — Mr. Standfast was inspired. Because of him, our choir was famous throughout London, and the old masters,

Handel (who had done so much for the hospital) and Mozart and Haydn, were as familiar to us as our friends. He had infinite patience, and he cared so much he made us care as well. No one was ever late for choir practice. No one ever fidgeted or whispered. He spread a golden net around us and drew us in.

On Sundays and at special concerts four professional singers joined us: Miss Hackett, Miss Phebbs, Mr. Cantarella and Mr. Evans. But our choirmaster told us ("and you must never let it out, my dears, that I said this") that it was our voices the audience came to hear.

When I sang, when I was surrounded by others singing, when I watched Mr. Standfast's baton and threw my whole heart into the music, my misery dropped away, the walls of the hospital fell flat and the iron gates melted, and my spirit was free. The long sermons, the awful Foundling Hymn, the hated uniforms, none of them mattered. My soul soared and I was full of joy. I held on to that feeling — or tried to — for the rest of the day.

Such strange Sundays, looking back — a mixture of Heaven and Hell. I could understand that boy, Jeremiah Brown, choosing his cornet over his mother.

One of the girls, Mavis Carboy, was blind; she wore a green band over her eyes. The story was that her mother had dosed her with laudanum before she was brought in, so the apothecary, who did not wish to wake her, never examined her eyes. Perhaps because of her blindness, the Creator had given her an exquisite voice, just as He had given Grandfather the gift of seeing with his hands. She was older than me by a few years, nearly old enough to leave, but who, we wondered, would take her? Where would she go?

At practice she stood with her hands clasped in front of her while Mr. Standfast played the melody over and over until she had it by heart. Then we all learned the words by rote; she was often quicker than the rest of us. Once, when we were practising *Messiah*, and Mavis's voice soared so effortlessly up to the high notes, Mr. Standfast said, with tears in his eyes, "The people that walk in darkness have seen a great light."

Once, when Miss Hackett was in hospital with a burst appendix, Mavis was allowed to sing a solo. The Governors were furious and Mr. Standfast nearly lost his post because of it.

"But they know better than to dismiss him," said Amy. "It's solely because of him that so many fashionable people rent pews in the chapel."

"Not *solely*," Caroline said. "They also come to stare at us."

"That novelty would soon wear off," Amy said, "if it weren't for our splendid music. They'd be fools to let him go."

"But what will become of Mavis when she leaves here? Will she stand on a street corner singing for coppers?"

"The Governors would never allow that. Somebody will think of something."

Nurse Gaynor, who slept at the end of our ward, had two nephews who sometimes came to visit her. One day the older of the two walked through the ward while we were dressing. We immediately turned our backs on him. I don't know where Nurse was, or why he chose to stop by my bed, but he did.

"Turn around," he said, but I remained as still as a statue.

"Turn around, whatever yer name is."

I did not move.

He grabbed my shoulder as though to turn me, and I wheeled around and hit him in the face.

He yelled and the other girls cheered, and Nurse came running, horrified to find her "nevvy" on the ward. She dragged him away, a satisfying stream of blood gushing from his nose.

And then she came back to plead with us not to tell. I was still shaking with outrage.

"It were all a mistake, he took a wrong turning."

"He touched me," I said.

"He never did."

"They all saw it. Why do you think I hit him?" My shoulder still burned where he had dared to put his hand on my bare flesh.

"I suggest," said Amy to Nurse, "that you start packing."

Oh how she pleaded with us, and oh how we stood there in our shifts, as cold as statues.

We were late going down to breakfast and Matron came to see what was wrong.

"You will go *now*," she told the trembling woman, "and take your nephews with you. You will not work here another minute. And you will go without a character, God help you."

That night we had no nurse, and Matron, distraught, trusted us to look after ourselves.

"She's upset," Amy said, "because she is in charge of hiring the female staff. In the end, she's responsible for what happened. She may go as well."

We liked Matron and felt relieved that it didn't come to that.

The other girls on the ward considered me something of a heroine, but I felt no triumph, just a terrible anger at the way I had been treated. Although they wanted to whisper all night, I crawled into bed and turned my face away. I kept hearing his ugly voice: "Turn around, whatever yer name is." He spoke to me as though I were nothing, and it came home to me that day that there might be men who would always see me that way in the outside world. I was thirteen years old, and this was the knowledge that made me turn my face to the wall.

The sewing mistress, who was lame, took a liking to me because, thanks to my foster mother, I was clever with my needle. She taught me to tat, and I took to it so quickly I was soon making doilies and runners and edgings for collars and cuffs. These she sent to a shop in Southampton Row, along with knitted goods and other items made in sewing class. She could not pay us — that was not allowed — but she would often, towards the end of class, produce a bag of sweets and pass them out. One Christmas she gave each of us a sugar mouse.

She was our youngest mistress and quite pretty. We thought she was wasted at the hospital in spite of her nice bed-sitting room and the lavender scent on her handkerchiefs on Sundays. Phoebe was sure that she had a tragic background, and indeed she had a slight air of melancholy that suggested something mysterious in her past. Caroline thought she was probably a clergyman's daughter, one of a large family, and did not wish to be a governess or work in a shop. Being lame would make it hard for her to stay on her feet all day.

"But if she worked in a shop, she would meet people."

By people, of course, we meant men.

Sometimes I was invited into her parlour to look at a new tatting pattern and take a cup of tea. She had a lovely embroidered shawl thrown over a table, always a small bunch of flowers in a vase and real beeswax candles, which smelled heavenly when lit.

She gave me a crochet hook and showed me how to join up the circles, making the edgings even more interesting, and I loved to lean near her and study her long, fine fingers as they demonstrated a stitch.

The other girls in our ward teased me and said I was her pet, but they were just jealous and knew better than to tease me too far.

When Mother came next — so lovely and familiar in her old bonnet and shawl — I showed her my shuttle and crochet hook and presented her with a collar with a fancy edge. She had changed a good deal since the boys had gone, and her hair was now completely grey. There had been only one letter from Sam, in all the years, and from Jonnie she had heard nothing. Her voice trembled when she spoke of her sons.

"Is it all right here, Hattie? Are you resigned to it now?"

"Never resigned, Mam, but I suppose I've got used to it." I told her about my special friends, Caroline, Amy and Phoebe, and about the music master and the girl who was blind like Grandfather, except that she had been blind from birth.

"God takes away," she said, "but He gives back."

I couldn't see what he had given back to her — all those dead babies in the churchyard and her living children gone forever.

"I love you, Hattie," she said as she was leaving. "We all love you. Never doubt it for one minute."

All my bravado vanished and I threw myself into her arms and wept.

Grandfather was dead; I would never see him again in this life.

"Why, Harriet, you're crying," said Nurse. "I never thought I'd see the day."

"Leave her alone," said Amy. "Have you no heart?"

I have not mentioned boys. We saw them, of course, on Sundays, at choir practice and at their end of the playground, but we were not supposed to speak to them. They ate in a separate dining hall and slept in a different wing. Boys grew up to be men and men had got our mothers into trouble. When Matron talked to us about such things, she was very severe. Kind as she was, I believe that in her heart she thought that, given our origins, we had a natural tendency to stray from the beaten path. Thus it was up to her, now that we were becoming women, to strike the fear of men into our hearts. We would have a harder time than most, she hinted, and must always be on guard. Once we left the hospital and were engaged as domestic servants, we would have days off, or at least half-days off, and we should be planning ahead what we would do with such idleness. We must never talk to strangers, we must walk briskly, backs straight, eyes straight ahead. It would help to carry a Bible.

Never touch spirits or go to coffee rooms. Beware of soldiers, especially officers. And sometimes the master of the house, or one of the elder sons . . . Her voice trailed away, but her face spoke clearly.

"I expect I shall sleep on my time off," Amy said.

"It's all so ridiculous," Caroline said. "Look at us. Why would anyone give us a second glance?"

"We won't always be wearing these awful brown uniforms."

"No, we'll be wearing awful black ones instead."

"Unless we marry," Phoebe said.

"And who are we to marry? Do you want to marry the bootboy or the groom? Servants marry servants, that's the way of the world."

We were all so depressed by this fact that we went straight to sleep.

Older girls and boys left to serve their apprenticeships; the babies kept arriving. We sewed little nightgowns and wondered if we would ever have children of our own. Meanwhile, we learned everything it would be useful for a servant in a small family to know. We scrubbed and blacked stoves and grates and learned how to lay a good fire and how to scatter tea leaves on carpets to keep them fresh. How to turn sheets and make a French seam down the middle. How to prepare nursery food in case we ever rose to positions as nursery nurses. Which soothing syrups were safe for Baby and which weren't. Above all, how to do all these things quickly and quietly, not raising dust or clattering up and down stairs like an Irish slattern.

"We are proud of the reputation of our Foundling girls and boys," Matron said. ("Hattie, you have blacking on your nose, that won't do.") "You must strive to live up to that reputation."

The blind girl had gone; Mr. Standfast had come up with a solution; he married her. She was never allowed to sing in the chapel again, but she was safe. We imagined them giving small concert parties where people would come to marvel at her voice, or we imagined them practising duets together, their voices blending perfectly. We never imagined them kissing.

Our domestic lessons continued. We carried heavy cans of water up and down the back stairs, heavy trays of crockery. Matron taught us a little bobbing curtsy and how to snuff a candle without letting it smoke. "Always use the candle snuffer, girls, *do not* lick your fingers and snuff the candle that way."

And one day, Mr. Brownlow called me down to the court room. There was a gentleman with him, quite a young man, shortish, with a bright embroidered waistcoat under his coat.

"Harriet," Mr. Brownlow said, "do you know who this man is?"

The other gentleman smiled at me; my heart began to gallop.

"My father, sir?"

After a moment the other one threw back his head and roared with laughter.

"Oh Lor'," he said, wiping his eyes with a handkerchief. "Oh my."

I hung my head; I hated being laughed at. Even Mr. Brownlow was laughing.

"No, no, child, this is Mr. Dickens. He has come to engage you as a servant. He is a regular attendant at chapel on Sunday and takes a keen interest in all that goes on here. I think you could not ask for a better placement."

For a moment I felt like that boy Jeremiah Brown must have felt. I didn't want to leave the known, however detested, for the mysterious unknown. But I had no choice, of course. It wasn't a case of cornet over unknown mother.

When I raised my eyes to the strange man's face, he was smiling at me so kindly that I forgave him at once for laughing and returned his smile.

"My wife," he said, "has not been well these past months, which is why I am here instead of Mrs. Dickens. However, day to day, you will be responsible to her. We have one child, the prettiest boy in all England, and there will be another child in the autumn. Your role will be that of housemaid, with some duties in the nursery. My wife is a sweet, gentle woman, but not strong. Are you strong, Harriet?"

I thought of the practice with the heavy cans of water, the trays of crocks, up the stairs and down, up the stairs and down. I reckoned I was stronger than he was, even allowing for the fact that he was a man, but of course I didn't say so.

"Yes, sir."

"And of an even temper? Not given to hysterics?"

"Yes, sir. No, sir."

"Then I think you will do very well."

Mr. Brownlow nodded and smiled. "Excellent. Excellent. And," he added, "Harriet is famous for her needlework."

Mr. Dickens did not seem very interested in my needlework.

I was taken away by Matron and given a small parcel containing two new frocks, two nightgowns, two shifts, a bonnet, a cloak and a new pair of shoes. I took off my uniform, apron and cap and put on one of the frocks. The rest of my clothes were packed in a small trunk, along with some examples of my fancywork and, of all things, the little handkerchief baby that had been taken away from me so long ago. The sewing mistress left her class to come and press into my hands a beautiful ivory shuttle and some new instruction booklets on tatting and crochet.

"Come and see me next year, Hattie, and write and tell me how you are getting on."

I felt quite sorry for her at that moment, stuck at the Foundling until she died. Whatever fate awaited me, it had to be better than that.

One last look at my iron bed, at the rows of iron beds and

the high, barred windows, and then the ward was locked again. Who would sleep in my bed tonight? Would I be missed?

I was not allowed to say goodbye to my friends but went back downstairs with Matron, who said she would arrange for the carting of my trunk. It was so small and contained so little I felt I could carry it myself, but that would not have been seemly.

"Are we ready then?" my employer said.

"There is just one thing more, a formality we must go through with all our children as they leave to go out in the world."

The formality consisted of a short sermon Mr. Brownlow read out to me, how I must always be a credit to the Hospital and so on, but I must confess I did not pay much attention, so anxious was I to be gone. Then I was given a handshake and the gift of a Holy Bible and Book of Common Prayer, and, that done, Mr. Dickens and I walked out the main door and across the grounds. Through the open window I could hear the Infant School saying their times tables: "Two twos is four, three twos is six, four twos is eight . . ." The porter opened the great gates, and for the first time in my life I stepped out onto a London street.

"We should walk," said my new employer. He smiled at me; I was nearly as tall as he was. "Are you surprised there is no carriage?"

I nodded; I was surprised.

"Well, my house is a mere stone's throw away from here, so we shall walk. It will take no more than five minutes."

I hid my disappointment. I was hoping to go far away, to another part of London altogether, and here I was to be right around the corner! But at least I was out. I took great gulps of air, dizzy with the thought.

"Do you like to walk, Harriet?"

"I don't really know, sir."

"What do you mean?"

"We girls did not go outside the grounds, sir, but I expect I shall like walking very much."

"I walk every day," he said. "London is a capital city for walking. There is so much to see."

A few yards down Guildford Street we turned right into a small street with a gate across it. A very fat boy dressed in a dark red uniform came out of the lodge to let us in. He stared at me hard and then winked.

"I chose this street because it is so very quiet," Mr. Dickens said. "No vans rattling up and down and so forth. I need absolute quiet for my work."

"Yes, sir," I said, although I had no idea what he was talking about. Oh well, I knew how to be quiet; I had had much training in *that*.

A few houses up, on the left, he stopped in front of a green door, set back a few feet from the street. He took out a key and motioned me forward.

"And this," he said, with an elaborate gesture, "is me 'umble 'ome" — he paused — "and now yours."

We entered a narrow hallway, where he placed his hat on a hall tree and went to the foot of the stairs.

"Kate," he bellowed, "she's here!"

4

I was never a servant but in that one household, so I can't really say what it was like elsewhere, but through talking to other servants, it seems to me that the Dickens household was very different, chiefly because of Mr. Dickens, who was unlike any man I have met before or since. For one thing, he shut himself up in his study half the day, writing books. I suppose I knew that real people wrote books — weren't Matthew, Mark, Luke and John real people? wasn't John Bunyan? — but I assumed they were all dead. It seemed such a queer occupation for a man, to sit by himself for hours, making things up. And to get paid — paid handsomely — for what amounted to day-dreaming. Nobody else thought it strange, quite the opposite in fact, and the house catered to his peculiar obsession. He was never to be disturbed when he was writing, and we must all go about on tiptoe. Once Mr. Dickens heard me singing as I was hanging up clothes in the garden (his study was at the back). Suddenly a window flew open and he shouted down at me, "Beware of blackbirds! Stop that racket!" I was so startled, I dropped the sheet and had to rinse it all over again.

But once he had finished work for the day, he was a different man, noisy, full of fun, bellowing and teasing or presiding at dinners where the sauce was always laughter. He could imitate just about anyone: soldiers, sailors, barrow men, the Prime Minister even. He loved to pretend he was a drunken district commissioner in some far-off place, India or Africa, giving the toast to the Queen or to Absent Friends, mixing up his words and finally sliding under the table. When I was asked to help Cook serve and remove, I had a terrible time to keep from laughing.

He loved practical jokes. One day he came to the back door dressed as an old Jew, in a long, dirty overcoat and with a long, straggly beard. I recognized him at once, but he gave me a look, and so I kept quiet while Cook chased him away with her rolling pin, shouting she'd "old rag" him, and how in mercy's name did he get past the gate at the end of the road? Oh, it was so comical; I had a pain in my side from laughing so hard.

When Cook found out that she had been hoodwinked, she was not pleased and threatened to give in her notice. I decided it would be wise not to mention that I had seen through the disguise (his eyes gave him away, squint though he would), but it did bring home to me, yet again, how our dress defines us. At the hospital we were more than four hundred separate young souls, with hair in every range of colour and eyes of every hue. Yet to the fashionable ladies who came to see us on Sundays, we were just "boy foundling" or "girl foundling." That was our identity.

And the fat young man who guarded the gate into Guildford Street loved to whisper to me, "Orfink, Orfink, oh yes, we knows *you*!" every time I passed in or out. He knew I had come from the hospital; he knew I would always wear that uniform, whatever my clothing. He had a fat sister who brought him his dinner from the public house in Lamb's Conduit Street. Mr. Dickens enjoyed talking to him. "I declare, that boy sweats gravy!" he said, and — I did not understand this at the time —

"I conjure them up and then, by God, they appear in real life! I must be more careful."

The house in Doughty Street consisted of four floors, the household of eight persons: Mr. and Mrs. Dickens; Mr. Dickens's younger brother Fred; the Dickens's little boy Charley, who was not yet eight months old; Cook; the nursemaid, who left about a month after I arrived; William, the groom, who lived over the stables in Doughty Mews; and myself. Cook was uneven in temper and liked port, the nursemaid gave herself airs, and William I rarely saw except when he brought a horse round for Mr. Dickens to go out riding to Richmond with one of his friends. When I went there first, I slept with Cook in a little closet off the kitchen, but later, after the nursemaid left — dismissed for having a follower — I slept in a garret room across from Fred and next to the nursery and, until the next baby came, more or less took over the care of Charley, as well as doing my regular tasks. This was the first time in my life I had ever slept in a room alone, and in the beginning it unnerved me. I felt like the only chick in a nest, and I even missed Cook's snores. But gradually I came to look forward to retreating to my little room at the end of a long day, and when I couldn't sleep — I learned that one can be too tired to sleep — I opened my window, which looked down on to Doughty Street, and leaned on the sill, listening to the faraway roar of those parts of the city which never really slept, or not until the last hours of the night, and heard the chimes of St. Paul's: one o'clock, dong; two o'clock, dong dong; and the halves and quarters in between. Sometimes I wondered if Jonnie were out there somewhere, listening as well, or whether Sam in Australia ever looked up at the moon that looked down upon us all.

There had been a sister of Mrs. Dickens — Mary — who had

died suddenly in May. Cook said that it was a terrible tragedy because everyone loved her and she was just seventeen. Mr. Dickens wore her ring on his little finger. Her sister's death on top of her advancing pregnancy seemed to make Mrs. Dickens somewhat melancholy. Often, when I took Charley down to her after his nap, I could see that she had been crying. She was always very kind to me, and I was truly sorry when I heard later what had happened to her.

She brightened when Mr. Dickens came into the room — we all did. He was such a whirlwind of energy and liveliness it was hard not to smile when he was downstairs. And he bestowed funny nicknames on everyone — he called baby Charley "Flasher Phoby," I don't know why. But he could be very strict. He had a place for everything and could not bear disorder. Mrs. Dickens told me that even when he travelled, he would rearrange his rooms until they suited him. She said he had such charm the landladies never objected.

Various relations came to dinner, but with one exception I didn't know any of them well enough to form an opinion. Cook said Mr. Dickens's father was a trial and he expected too much from his son, but then, she said, now that he was famous, the whole world had its hand in his pocket.

"Is he very famous, Cook?"

"Oh Lord, yes, and gettin' famouser by the minute. And him such a young man, too, not yet thirty."

On Sunday Mr. Dickens went to chapel at the Foundling; Mrs. Dickens accompanied him if she felt well enough. One day he invited me to go, for Mr. Brownlow had told him I liked music and sang in the choir. I thanked him but told him no. I had no desire to go back through those iron gates until the obligatory visit the next Whitsuntide.

"I am concerned about your spiritual health, Harriet." I felt that he was teasing me.

"I read my Bible, sir, and I say my prayers."

"Wouldn't you like to go for the music?"

"No, sir." (Even so, it was the one thing about the place I missed, and I often sang quietly to Charley or to myself when I was in my room.)

On my half-day I put on my new bonnet and shawl and went out of Doughty Street and into the wide world, the fat boy in his ridiculous livery whispering, "Oh yes, we knows *you*," from where he sat on his stool. I always walked on the other side of the street as I passed the hospital and headed for Southampton Row. I did not dawdle, but I observed everything — the multitudes of men and women hurrying along, going from somewhere to somewhere else, the carriages of the fashionable ladies, the nursemaids in Russell Square chatting to one another as their precious charges ran about on the paths, the hawkers of fruit and vegetables, of oysters and pies. The boardmen along Tottenham Court Road advertising chop houses, plays, patent medicine. Once I even saw a procession of huge portmanteaux and boxes proceeding down Oxford Street, followed by a group of laughing boys. I thought for a minute I had lost my senses, but it was really a parade of men with only heads and legs sticking out, advertising a trunk maker. The boys were abusing them, shouting at them and shoving, trying to knock them over. The sight was comical in the extreme, but the boardmen did not look happy; I never saw one that did. They could not stand still, like the costermongers or flower sellers, but had to be forever on the move.

Always I looked for Jonnie; I felt sure I should recognize him if I saw him, even after all this time.

Sometimes men spoke to me, but something in my manner must have dissuaded them from following.

There were many beggars, often dressed in bits of soldiers' apparel, but Cook told me she'd eat a fish head if any of them had done service anywhere but in a pub.

I walked miles and miles, sometimes as far as Kensington Gardens, sometimes down to the river, always listening for the church bells so I would not be late returning home. I never went to the very poor areas around Seven Dials; Mrs. Dickens had warned me that no girl should enter such places alone.

"Mr. Dickens goes, but he is a grown man. Nevertheless, I even fret about him sometimes, although I know he must because of his work."

The freedom to move about, the freedom not to be one drab child in a host of drab children. On washdays, when I helped the washerwoman with the family wash and my hands became rough and raw from the soda and scalding water; on days when Charley had been fractious and I had to sit up half the night with him and still be up before dawn to light the fires and heat water; on days when nothing seemed to go right — then I grumbled a little to myself, but really, I felt so free compared to my prison life at the hospital that my grumbling did not last long.

One person, however, could always rub me the wrong way and reduce me to smouldering fury.

My single extravagance was stationery, for every fortnight I wrote a letter home to Father and Mother in Shere, describing my life on Doughty Street and the wonderful sights that I saw on my walks through London. I told them how well I was treated and how I prayed for them both every night and for Sam and Jonnie as well.

Until the penny post came in, I had to save enough to pay for the delivery of the letter, for I knew they would go without to pay the postage if I didn't.

I told them how noisy London was, once you got out into the crowded streets, and how often I thought of the music of the Tillingbourne as it rushed along and the song of the lark in the clear air. Sometimes my tears smeared the letters by the end, for I did sorely miss them and always would.

Mrs. Dickens had a young sister named Georgina. She was just a little girl, no more than ten or eleven when I first went into service in Doughty Street, but she had a sharp tongue and made pronouncements as though she were much older.

"*Who* is that girl?" I heard her say, shortly after I arrived. "Surely that is not the new housemaid?"

Mrs. Dickens said yes, that was indeed who I was.

"She looks like a gypsy, she looks like a girl not to be trusted."

She liked to call me Coram, unlike the rest of the household. Early on Mr. Dickens had suggested that I might prefer not to be called by the name of the Foundling's father and that I might prefer to be addressed as Harriet or Hattie.

Georgina was in and out of every room, always criticizing her older sister, digging at her in little ways, almost mocking her now that she was heavy and slow with her pregnancy. When I brought Charley down, she would grab him and say, "Thank you, Coram, you may go," as though *she* were the lady of the house.

And when Mr. Dickens was around, it was plain that she worshipped him. Of course he liked that and never really saw her other side. I had known one or two girls like her at the hospital, girls who took pleasure in criticizing others in subtle ways, goading them into bad behaviour or tears; girls with a mean streak, telltales as well, but who could be all sweetness and light when it suited them. They were usually favourites with the more gullible adults.

Twice Georgina nearly cost me my place. Mrs. Dickens could be slow and forgetful, whereas Miss Georgy was swift and clever and as keen on order as her brother-in-law. Once, when she came upon her sister crying (Mrs. Dickens had forgotten to do something important — decline or accept a dinner invitation — and this had led to some awkwardness), she said, "For heaven's sake, stop that crying. You know how Charles hates it when you cry. What's done is done, and crying won't make it any better."

A proper little madam, she could be. Very unchildlike.

One afternoon, she called me back just as I was leaving the parlour.

"Oh Coram, would you stop a moment please? I wish to ask your advice about something."

Sensing a trap, I returned reluctantly and stood in front of her. Mrs. Dickens smiled encouragement as she peeled an orange and fed slices of fruit to her son. He struggled to get down when he saw me come back; Charley and I got on very well. I shook my head at him and told him I would be back for him later. Miss Georgy watched this exchange with a little smirk. She removed a length of brown material from a large paper parcel by her chair.

"I have been invited to a fancy-dress party at the end of the month, and I decided it would be great fun to go as a Foundling Girl. Mama has bought the material but we have no pattern. I wonder, do you still have your old uniform by you?"

"No, Miss Georgy. I left it at the hospital."

"What a pity, but never mind, you can describe it for me

instead. I could ask Charles when he comes in, I know he goes to the chapel every Sunday, and he is so observant, but I do not like to trouble him with so trivial a matter."

I remained silent; I couldn't believe my ears.

"Well?" She had taken out a writing tablet and a pencil.

"I don't remember, Miss Georgy."

"You wore that outfit every day for ten years and you don't remember?"

"Yes, Miss Georgy."

She looked me full in the face. How she was enjoying this! My cheeks burned.

"I don't believe you."

I stared straight at her — insolent servant! — and said nothing. I may even have shrugged.

"Georgy," Mrs. Dickens said, "leave it, dear. You can ask Charles. He'll be down soon."

"I will *not* ask Charles. I will ask Coram, who for some strange reason refuses to reply. The material is already bought, as you can see, and I am determined to use it."

At that moment Charley reached for his mother's teacup, which she was just raising to her lips, grabbed it and would have tipped it over her frock if I hadn't darted forward and taken it from him.

"Kate," Miss Georgy said, "pay attention to what you are doing."

That was too much — this high and mighty little baggage with her superior airs. In my anger and frustration, and barely conscious of what I was doing, I threw the cup at the wall. Then I ran out of the room and up the stairs to the very top, to my room.

How dare she! To pose as a Foundling Girl at a party; to

wear once, and as a kind of joke, what I had had thrust upon me for ten years. And now I would be dismissed, I knew it, sent back to the hospital without a character, fit only to be a scullery maid or worse. And Matron and Mr. Brownlow, my family as well — disgracing myself before all those who had believed in me. I sobbed and sobbed.

It was Fred who tapped on my door an hour later.

"Hattie, Mr. Dickens wants to see you in his study."

I had never been in Mr. Dickens's study before; no one was allowed in unless invited and I assume he did the dusting himself. I was too upset to take in much, but I saw him look up from a table covered with slips of blue paper.

"Ah, Harriet. Come here, please. I understand you, ah, you broke a teacup."

"Yes, sir."

"I had not thought of you as clumsy."

"No sir, I am not, as a general rule."

"Then how came the teacup to be broken? Did you really throw it against the wall?"

"Yes, sir."

"Would you care to tell me why? I understand you rescued it from Charley. Why rescue it if you were going to destroy it a moment later?"

I did not wish to answer; it would be Miss Georgy's word against mine, a servant against a sister-in-law.

He moved a little china monkey from one end of the table to the other, back and forth. "Look at me, Harriet."

"Yes, sir."

"You have nothing more to say on this matter? You are not going to try and defend yourself. Whine or cry?"

I shook my head.

"You know, I must write to Mr. Brownlow soon, for I gave my word I would keep him informed. What am I to say to him?"

I could feel the traitor tears beginning, but I dug my nails into my palm and forced them down.

"Very well. You may go."

A tear slid down my cheek, but he pretended not to notice.

"Go where, sir?"

"Why, back to work. What on earth did you think I meant?"

At this the tears poured down; I could not stop them. I searched blindly for the door, but he got up and put his hand on my shoulder.

"Listen to me, Hattie. Never be ashamed of where you came from, never. But mind your temper. If something provokes you — and I suspect Miss Georgy did not mean to provoke you — count to two and twenty before you begin smashing the china. Will you promise me that?"

I couldn't speak; I could only nod.

"Two and twenty, remember?"

I nodded again.

"Say it."

"Yes, sir. Two and twenty."

"Good girl."

Cook told me later that she had eavesdropped behind the parlour door and that I had caused a great uproar. Miss Georgy wanted me dismissed and "sent back to where she came from," but Mrs. Dickens defended me and said how good I was with Charley, how much she had come to depend on me. She said Miss Georgy must have touched a nerve when she brought up the subject of the Foundling uniform, that perhaps I had taken the whole thing too much to heart. She and Mrs. Dickens had quite a set-to about it, but then Mr. Dickens came in and agreed with his wife, that I might have felt mocked or made fun of. He was quite severe with Miss Georgy, much to Cook's surprise.

"But you minds how you goes, my girl, you've made an henimy of that one. And I don't think as Master will be so forgiving a second time."

That evening I went to apologize to Mrs. Dickens.

"We will say no more about it, Hattie, but remember that Mr. Dickens likes a smooth-running household. He doesn't take kindly to disorder or disruption."

That night I prayed hard that God would help me to be a better person, and I vowed I would count to four and forty, eight and eighty, even, before I would ever be tempted to do such a thing again. I had had a very narrow escape.

No one ever mentioned the incident afterwards, but one day, when Miss Georgina was putting on her bonnet in the hall and I had just come in from my half-day off, she stopped me.

"Tell me, Coram, do you understand whom you are working for? Mr. Dickens is a very unusual man, a genius. The whole world will soon be talking of him. He can't stand uproars; he *must* have peace and quiet. Sometimes I don't think my sister understands that as well as I do. And now with another baby imminent."

She gave a dramatic sigh.

"He's a *genius*, Coram, and don't you ever forget it. *Your* feelings don't count, your little moods."

"Yes, Miss Georgina."

I wanted to ask her if she had enjoyed the fancy-dress party, but I counted to two and twenty and carried on up the stairs.

Mary was born on the sixth of March, 1838. I hadn't known about the screaming; I thought my mistress was going to die. Mr. Dickens's mother, who was staying with us for the confinement, came down to the kitchen, where I was sitting with Cook and Charley and warming soft cloths by the stove. I had carried up can after can of water, hot and cold, with Mrs. Dickens lying in the big bed, all the colour bleached out of her face. Even her lips were white.

"Is Charley all right?" she whispered.

"Charley is fine, ma'am. He's down in the kitchen with Cook and me, in the warm."

"But not too near the stove! He could burn himself on the stove!"

"It's all right. We tied him to the table leg with a bit of clothesline. He can move about, but he can't get near the stove."

"Hattie, thank you . . . bless you . . . you are such a help to me."

And then her face twisted with pain and she cried out.

Her torment went on for hours and hours. We could hear her screams all the way down to the bottom of the house. Mrs. Dickens Senior had sent for the doctor; the baby was stuck.

"Is she going to die?"

"Of course not, you silly goose. We all 'ave to bring forth in sorry, the Bible tells us so."

"But you heard her, the baby is stuck!"

"Doctor will turn it."

Mr. Dickens, once the pain began, had called for his horse and ridden off to Richmond with his friend Mr. Forster.

Charley had had his supper by now and had fallen asleep on my lap. I didn't dare move him, so I carefully brought out my tatting shuttle and thread and began some new edging. I had made some lovely nightgowns for the new baby, but now I was working on a collar and cuffs for my mother. Cook had served us both with some cold meat, bread and pickle, and now she helped herself to a tot of port.

The screams stopped.

"She's dead," I said, "I knew it."

"Nonsense. Wait and see."

After a while Mr. Dickens's mother came smiling into the kitchen with a bundle of bloody sheets. She saw her sleeping grandson and whispered, "It's a wee girl. Now they have a pigeon pair." She asked Cook to warm some beef tea.

"It was a hard one, that?"

"Very hard. She tore. But she's all smiles now."

"Yes, we soon forgets the pain, that's Nature's way. Other-wise nobody'd ever 'ave a second one." They smiled at one another and nodded.

Cook said she knew a cousin whose baby was stuck so bad and they pulled so hard that its little leg came off in the midwife's hands.

Mrs. Dickens put the bloody sheets to soak in cold water, then asked me to carry Charley upstairs and sit by him until called. I was dripping with sweat and feeling faint. So that was what it was like to bear a child — "The baby was stuck"; "She tore"; "Its little leg came off in the midwife's 'ands." Screams and bloody sheets. I would never let that happen to me.

The front door slammed and Mr. Dickens went pounding up the stairs; he had met the doctor on his way home. I heard his mother come out of the bedroom. "Hush, hush, they are both asleep."

Later, Cook and I were invited to see the new baby. My mistress was still pale, but she had a glow on her and looked very young and happy. The baby was in a cradle by the bed. I had seen hundreds of little babies at the Foundling, for I was one of the trusted big girls who stood with babies in their arms while the chaplain sprinkled them with water and gave them new names. "In the name of the Father . . ."

This was different. Mr. Dickens was sitting close up to the bed, holding his wife's hand, beaming.

"She is to be called Mary," he said, "after the dearest, sweetest girl who ever lived." I thought this remark a bit peculiar, given the hell my mistress had just been through, but she smiled and nodded.

"Yes, after Mary, but I think we shall call her Mamie amongst ourselves."

The baby was just another baby, red-faced and wrinkled. What brought tears to my eyes was the sight of the happy family: father, mother, newborn *wanted* child.

We offered our congratulations and stole away.

By the new year she was pregnant again.

5

"Writing to your sweetheart, Coram?"

Miss Georgina often appeared in the kitchen without warning, hoping to catch us stuffing our faces with forbidden foods or entertaining riffraff. It drove Cook wild.

"I am writing to my mother," I said, without looking up.

"Your *mother*?"

"My foster mother, then."

"What a good girl you are, the very model of a foster daughter."

Miss Georgina had come down to ask Cook, as a special request from Mrs. Dickens, if she could make a Madeira cake and some flapjack because the family were coming to tea. Cook scowled, but of course she would do it.

At the door Miss Georgy turned and addressed me once more.

"Oh, Coram, can your foster mother read?"

"Of course she can," I lied. "Why?" (Count to two and twenty, count to two and twenty, one, two, three, four . . .)

"I'm rather surprised, that's all. How long has it been since you saw her?"

"Over a year, but I shall see her soon."

"How so?"

"I'm to go home for a few days around Easter."

"My goodness! Kate — your mistress — can let you go when there is so much to do here?"

Cook stopped on her way to the larder.

"Mrs. Hogarth — your mother — will be coming to visit for a few days. It's all arranged, Miss Georgina."

"Is it now? I have not heard of it. And Mrs. Hogarth is not a nursemaid. How typical of soft-hearted, soft-headed Kate!"

Cook spoke up for me.

"It's in the contract, Miss Georgy. The girl gets three days off each year to go and see her mother."

"Well, you are a lucky girl. I shouldn't think many servant girls have such agreements with their employers."

Smirk, smirk and she was gone.

"I'll flapjack 'er," Cook said. "The sooner she's growed up and married off and 'as a 'ousehold of 'er own to manage, the better for everybody."

"She's never going to marry. I heard her say that to Madam."

"That's unnatcherl. She'll change 'er mind when she's a little older."

"Why does she dislike me so?"

"Well, I don't think it's because of your curly hair. I thinks it's because Master likes you. I thinks it's because *she'd* like to be living 'ere."

I folded my letter and prepared to go back upstairs to the nursery. Charley was with his mother, being specially dressed up for his relatives in a new little sailor suit. The baby was asleep.

"Mrs. Rogers," I said (I never called her Cook to her face), "when the time comes, would you teach me how to make a simnel cake? I've been saving for the spices and such. Mrs. Dickens suggested I should take one to my mother when I go."

Cook looked up from where she was cracking eggs one-handed into a big bowl.

"Of course, love. I'll 'elp yer make the best cake you've never seen."

In the end, Mrs. Dickens said she wanted to help as well. And oh, what fun we had, with Cook's big aprons tied around our middles, our arms dusty with flour. Carefully we measured out the cloves, the cinnamon, the currants and sultanas. Carefully we whisked together the eggs, sugar and butter. Oh so carefully we poured half the mixture into the tin, laid a circle of marzipan on the top, added the remaining batter.

"If you make a shallow well in the centre, Hattie, your cake will rise evenly."

As we waited for the cake to bake, Mrs. Dickens sat down at the big kitchen table, just as though she were one of us, drank a cup of tea from a kitchen mug and helped herself to the tarts Cook had baked that morning.

"I shouldn't," she said. "I'll get thick in the waist."

There was the lovely smell of cake and the sound of rain falling outside the kitchen window. Mrs. Hogarth had come early to supervise in the nursery, and Mr. Dickens and Fred had gone out on some family business. The three of us sat together in a little island of peace.

"What is she like, Hattie, your foster mother?"

"Small," I said, smiling. "I am now much taller than she is. She has grey hair, although she is still not old, and freckled skin. When we were little and grew restless, she would sit us down and ask us to try and count the freckles on one arm. Since we could never count beyond ten, we would have to begin all over again."

"We?"

"Her son Jonnie, ma'am, my foster brother. And then there was an older brother as well, Samuel."

I was still smiling as I said this, but the tears stood in my eyes as I thought of Sam and Jonnie.

She laid her hand upon my arm.

"Mr. Brownlow told Mr. Dickens something of your brothers' history. I'm sorry, I had forgotten. Perhaps it will all come right in the end."

"Perhaps."

"You were very happy there?"

I nodded. "Very."

When the cake was done, tested with a straw and declared to be perfect — the whole kitchen full of its fragrance — we put it in the larder to cool, and Mrs. Dickens and I went up to relieve her mother of the children. Miss Georgina was coming to tea, alas, but since her mother would be there, and her older sister Helen, I did not expect any pert remarks when I brought the children down to the parlour. I was to leave the next morning for Shere, and what with the lovely interlude of cake-baking and the thought of my coming journey, I was in the happiest of moods.

Charley, at fourteen months, was a wriggler and hated being confined in fussy clothes. He would lie on his face on the nursery rug and refuse to sit up. It was all a game, really, and I had learned that if I ignored him and started to dress Mamie, muttering, "Oh dear, what a pity Charley isn't going down, and there are butter tarts for tea," he soon came round. Mamie was different right from the start — a smiler. You could do anything with Mamie.

Charley did not want to hold on to me as we went downstairs, but the stairs were steep and I insisted, muttering, "Oh dear, oh dear, butter tarts and jam sponge," and refusing to go on until he did as he was told.

Miss Georgina had arrived; I could hear her voice as we descended the last flight.

"You spoil her!"

My mistress's voice was low, so I could not hear her reply.

Then Miss Georgy again: "She is a *servant*, Kate. You have no notion of how to treat servants."

My mistress laughed. I knocked and brought the children in just as she said, "Well, you'll have some of your own one day, and then you can play the lady."

Charley headed straight for his mother and claimed her lap so there would be no room for Baby. I went over and, placing Mamie on the sofa, whispered in Charley's ear, "Oh dear, oh dear, butter tarts and jam sponge," whereupon he promptly got down and went over to his grandmother.

"What a nice big brother you are," Mrs. Hogarth exclaimed, and I left the children to the adoring women, after making sure that the tea trolley was set up and all that was needed was boiling water.

While the kettle boiled in the kitchen, I wrapped the cake in parchment paper and then again in heavy brown paper, ready for the morning.

Mothering Sunday being the fourth Sunday in Lent, Mr. Dickens said he had discussed it with his wife and they both thought I should be given the Monday off as well, so that I could have my three full days away, arriving back in London on the Tuesday evening.

I rose very early the next morning and tiptoed down the stairs to the kitchen in my stockinged feet, having left my shoes and my outer things on a chair there the night before. I quietly

made up the fire, removed the cake from the larder and put it in
my basket. My mistress had given me a lovely broad blue ribbon
to tie around it once I got home. Cook, who came out of her
closet just as I was leaving, handed me a packet of bread and
cheese, an onion and a stone bottle of ale. She warned me not
to talk to strange men. I was so happy I kissed her, which
surprised us both.

I walked through the quiet London streets, still shining from
yesterday's rain, and over the bridge to take the coach to Guildford. After that I would walk the six miles home. Because it was
Sunday, there was not much traffic and we made good time.
The coachman set me down just outside Guildford and pointed
me east towards Shere. Mr. Dickens, who was a great walker
himself, had consulted a gazetteer and drawn me a little map so
I should not get lost. He advised me not to tell "the ladies" I
intended to walk part of the way — "You know how ladies are."
He also gave me fourpence to stop at a public house, should I
become thirsty on my travels.

The March sun was warm, not hot, just right for walking,
and I disturbed no one as I walked along, smelling the sweet
smell of the ploughed fields after rain. During my long years in
London, I had forgotten what country air smelled like, and I
breathed deeply as I walked along, drinking it in like cool water.
And country scenes: young lambs in a meadow, a hare sitting
up in a field, an old white horse which trotted slowly up to greet
me over a fence. As I walked, I was accompanied by the piping
and the warbling of a blackbird. The road was not straight but
curved along below the rounded hills of the North Downs, and
I felt as though London were a hundred miles away, not less
than thirty.

There were times when I seemed to feel the presence of

someone beside me, a small girl in a faded blue dress, tugging impatiently at my shawl, enticing me to throw down my basket, rid myself of my shoes and come running across the fields with her to see what we could see. And oh, it was tempting, but I was a grown-up now, or nearly, with a situation and responsibilities; that little ghost-girl was no more than a dream of long ago.

Two tramps raised what was left of their hats to me, but they did not bother me or ask for money. However, I went on a bit before I spread my shawl on a dampish rock and stopped to eat my breakfast. I knew I should probably share — that would be the Christian thing to do — but I wanted to be alone, I was so enjoying my solitude. I thought to myself, "At this moment no one knows exactly where I am. No bells will ring save church bells, and should I meet any little children, they will be some-one else's."

After my meal, I did not have too far to walk before I rounded a corner and I was there. Past the Lodge and a new, handsome house nearby, past the Pound House and the cottage next to it . . . nearly running now . . . down Rectory Lane and across the stream at the ford (oh blessed, blessed music of that fast-flowing water) and into Lower Street, where our small cottage stood.

The bells of St. James began to ring just as I rushed through the open door. "Mother! Mother! I'm home" (even in my excite-ment, being careful to set down my basket with its surprise). "Oh Mother! Mother! Mother!"

She turned to me with a look of such joy it set me weeping as we ran to one another. "I'm home," I murmured, kissing the top of her head, "I'm home."

Hand in hand we made our way to the church, with Father, for once, following close behind. I was re-introduced to the

Misses Bray, who were gracious and asked questions; the rector shook my hand, and the women of the village — many, on this special Sunday, with daughters home — gathered round to greet me.

I looked carefully at the other girls, a few of whom were already married with a baby in their shawls, but most of whom were domestic servants in the big houses in Shere, Gomshall, Peaslake and Albury. Although their manners might be rougher than mine, and their speech also (living with Mr. and Mrs. Dickens had done wonders for my speech), I envied them their nearness to their families.

I saw the grave of my dear grandfather and spent a few minutes with the little dead babies, especially Hannah, whose place I had taken.

Back home, my mother exclaimed over the simnel cake and declared she had never seen anything so beautiful — it looked too good to eat.

I laughed. "Father and I will eat it then."

I gave her the new collar and cuffs, which of course looked "far too good for the likes of me," and gave my father a twist of tobacco, for Mother had told me he'd taken up the habit after Grandfather's death.

Mother kept wiping her eyes with her apron and saying she was being silly, then wiping her eyes again. She was overjoyed to hear I could stay for two nights.

"This must seem very small to you," Father said that evening, "this house, this village — after London."

"No, oh no. This is where my heart is. This is home."

In the spring of 1839, Mr. Dickens told me there was to be a grand concert at the Foundling to celebrate the one hundredth anniversary of the hospital. He and Mrs. Dickens and the Hogarths were taking tickets, and, he wondered, could he purchase a ticket for me?

"I know you sang in the chapel choir, Hattie, and Fred hears you singing in the nursery and in your room at night. I thought you might enjoy the concert; it will be selections from *Messiah*."

I did not hesitate. "Thank you, sir, but no."

"If you are worried about the children, Fred is not going, and since the concert is in the afternoon, he would be happy to keep an eye on them, I'm sure."

"I would rather not, thank you, sir."

I could see that he was not pleased with me, and I did not know how to explain without seeming ungrateful. My stomach churned just to think of going. It was not that I now thought of myself as above the children in the hospital — how could I? — but I tried not to dwell on my life there or why I had been admitted. Each time I reported to Mr. Brownlow at Whitsun and had to walk through those heavy gates, I was in such a state of agitation that I thought I would faint. It was ridiculous, I knew, for I was not really mistreated there and indeed had been a favourite of the sewing mistress. Perhaps I was afraid that once in, I would not get out again.

I felt so deeply about the place that still I always walked on the other side of the street on my way to Southampton Row. Sometimes I glanced across, briefly, at the statue of Thomas Coram, which towered over the entrance, and felt I owed him an apology for such revulsion. After all, I might have died in the workhouse if I had lived at all. So as much as I longed to hear the glorious music of *Messiah*, and to see my old choirmaster, I could not bring myself to go, even at the risk of offending Mr. Dickens.

I stopped at home and listened instead to the rumble of carriages down Guildford Street, the sound of horses' hooves, and cursed myself for a fool. Mrs. Dickens told me later that the concert had raised thousands of pounds for the hospital and that the singing was superb.

"There were carriages all the way down Southampton Row. We were fortunate that we could walk."

Miss Georgy had come back for tea. I heard her say something about the number of foundlings at the hospital, and how it never seemed to diminish, but she supposed there was some advantage to that, since it ensured a plentiful supply of servants, whatever it said about the stupidity of Woman.

"Ah, Georgy," said Mr. Dickens, "I don't think fallen women are to be considered some sort of natural resource for the supplying of servants to the well-to-do. That is a horrible thought and quite beneath you."

She was not used to being criticized by her brother-in-law and hastened to absolve herself.

"You are quite right; I was flippant. These women are more to be pitied than anything else, and the children must carry forever the mark of their mothers' shame."

"And fathers', Georgy, and fathers'."

"Oh, of course, and fathers'."

And then, as though seeing me for the first time (I was gathering up the plates and cups and saucers), she raised her finger to her lips and with a slight tilt of her head in my direction, said, "Shh, poor Coram is listening. We don't want to hurt her feelings."

(Two and twenty . . . two and twenty . . . two and twenty.)

6

Katie was born at the end of October. Once again, the delivery was hard and Mrs. Dickens recovered slowly. It was a fortnight before she came downstairs, and I could see that both her mother and Mr. Dickens were concerned about her. She had sudden fits of silent weeping and did not, for a while, express much interest in any of the children. I think Mamie sensed this and clung more and more to her father, when he was available. Charley, who was now rising three, did not seem to care much one way or the other. What he liked best was to ride his rock-inghorse on "adventures" or set up spirited battles with his box of lead soldiers. Occasionally Mr. Dickens would put him up on his own big horse and, with the groom on one side and himself on the other, walk him slowly up and down Doughty Mews. I was always commanded to come along and applaud. He had been promised a pony when he was old enough.

One day Mr. Dickens left his study door open and Charley ran in. I, of course, ran after him. I was amazed at the number of books on the shelves, and, forgetting that I was never to venture inside unless summoned, I was examining their titles when Mr. Dickens let out a roar behind me.

"What are you doing in here!"

"Charley ran in, sir, the door was open."

"Nonsense. I never leave the door open."

"Yes, sir."

Charley kicked against me, wanting down.

"Was it really open, Harriet, or did you just want to see the lion's den?"

"No, sir. It was open."

"Very well, I believe you." He smiled. "I see you have been looking at my books."

"Yes, sir."

"Would you like a book to read? From the way you were gazing at my books, I assume you are passionate about reading. You can read, Hattie?"

"Yes, sir. All the children at the Foundling are taught to read."

"How seditious. Will our servants remain content to do our drudgery if we teach them to read? What if they start to think for themselves?"

He smiled as he said this, so I knew it was a jest.

"I expect your taste runs to romance."

"Taste, sir?"

"Yes. What sort of reading do you fancy? Adventure, tragedy, romance, drama? Ah. Here." He handed me a book.

"Be very careful with this book. Keep it clean and out of the reach of this young man, who is a little too fierce with his own picture books, and never turn down the corners of the pages. When you finish that, come to me and perhaps I'll give you another."

I was so fatigued at night that my habit had been, except on my half-day off, to do a bit of tatting, say my prayers and fall asleep immediately. Now, no matter how tired I might feel, I lit my candle, and with a shawl around my shoulders I stayed up for an extra hour reading the wonderful book. It was *Robinson Crusoe*. I was amazed at how the hero contrived to exist on that hostile island, and so involved in the story was I that when Crusoe found the footprint in the sand, I actually cried out in terror and Fred came knocking on my door to see what was the matter.

When I finished that book, he gave me another and another and another. (But never, at that time, one he had written.)

One afternoon he said to me, as he handed me my latest book — *A Journal of the Plague Year*, also by Daniel Defoe — he said, "Hattie, how do you feel about children?"

"How do I feel about them, sir?"

"Yes. Do you like them?"

"I like them well enough. I'm particularly fond of the babies."

"I, too. I'm particularly fond of the babies. What a pity they can't be shot and stuffed before the age of five."

And once he said, "Do you think it odd, Harriet, the life I lead?"

"Odd, sir?"

"Yes, odd. While you are carrying cans of water up and down the stairs, dressing the children, managing the mangle, running errands, I sit shut up in my study, a man in his prime, making marks on slips of paper, or talking to myself, or pulling faces in the mirror. Do I appear to you as some sort of hermit, deliberately walled up here while life goes on outside?"

"No, sir."

"No, sir, what?"

"You do not seem a hermit." (I said nothing about "odd.") "And you come out of your cell in the afternoons."

"I come out of my cell in the afternoons! Oh Lor', that's wonderful. And then I greet real life head on, eh?"

"Yes, sir. And besides that . . ."

"Besides what?"

"Everyone knows you're a genius."

He positively bellowed with laughter, but I was used to him now; he didn't frighten me.

"Everyone? Who is this everyone?"

"Mrs. Dickens, sir. Her new maid, Cook, William Topping — everyone."

"Even the babies?"

"I'm not so sure about the babies."

"No, I wouldn't be so sure about the babies; I wouldn't count on those babies for endorsements in the genius department. In the providing of toys and sweets department, maybe."

After he dismissed me, I could hear him laughing and talking to himself. "I'm a genius. Everybody says so — Kate, the cook, the maid, the groom. But she's not sure about the babies. Oh wonderful, wonderful, wonderful."

Childlike himself, in so many ways. On Guy Fawkes night, just after Katie was born, he disappeared down to Southampton Row and persuaded a group of boys to let him black his face and join them. He went up and down the streets with them crying, "A penny for the Old Guy, a penny for the Old Guy."

"What larks," he told us later, "what fun."

He had had a leaning towards being a professional actor, he said, but on the day of his audition a sore throat had laid him low, and that was that. Now he entertained at dinner and convulsed everyone with laughter.

Such energy he brought to the house — he positively hummed with it, like a spinning top. Ran down the stairs, walked miles no matter what the weather, rode his horse, organized games at home or when we went down to Ramsgate for a holiday. (I did not like the sea, the way the waves kept coming and coming and coming, but he plunged right in and carried the children in as well. He called us cowardy custards if we refused to follow his example.)

Perhaps sitting in solitude for hours made him restless and talkative when he emerged. He loved to entertain, to be surrounded by people once his work was done, although an evening with his relatives sometimes brought him down. Once he said, "You know, Harriet, it's not such a bad thing to lack a pile of relations always looking for a favour, usually of a monetary nature."

Cook said he meant most particularly his father. "'Is father causes 'im a world of worry and trouble, 'e does."

But I imagined Mr. Dickens would not really like to be without his family, however much they annoyed him, just as Cook, now that her husband had "passed over," could refer to his drunkenness and bad habits with both scorn and affection.

The house on Doughty Street was now too small, so by Christmas of 1839 we were installed at Number One, Devonshire Terrace, near the York Gate entrance to Regent's Park. I, for one, was happy to move farther away from the shadow of the Foundling Hospital and the whispered taunts of the fat boy — "Orfink, orfink, oh yes, we know who *you* are!"

We had our first German tree that year, all lit up with tiny white candles; I don't think I have ever seen anything so lovely. The doors to the big parlour were kept closed until evening, the candles were lit, and then the entire household was ushered in. It was as though dozens of stars had descended on the big tree and nestled in its branches. And once the gas lamps were turned up, we could see little presents of toys and sweetmeats tied on the tree as well.

And the smell of the needles!

And the children's faces full of wonder and delight.

And Mr. Dickens, who had arranged the whole surprise, standing there grinning.

Mrs. Dickens seemed to regain some of her old cheerfulness with the move, and Cook said it was not just that she was feeling better "in 'er body" but that she was leaving the ghost of her dead sister behind.

"I saw 'em once," she said, "the Master, with 'is face in poor Mary's clothcs, weepin' like a little child. 'E were that fond of 'er. And she were a darling — as different from Miss Georgy as chalk from cheese. It were a tradegy when she died so sudden and so young. Everyone was haffected by hit. This 'ouse won't 'ave such melancholy memories."

Mr. Dickens's close friend Mr. Macready lived just down the way, so there was much to-ing and fro-ing over the holidays, and on Twelfth Night, which was Charley's birthday, a huge party. A rich lady, who was Charley's godmother, sent over a splendid Twelfth Night cake.

Mr. Dickens got the bean and Mrs. Macready the pea, so they were King and Queen and made everybody do ridiculous things, like stand on one leg for three minutes or recite a complicated sentence backwards. Even the servants had to join in, and when the King drank we all had to shout, "Lo, the King drinks!" or if the Queen ate something, "See where the Queen eats!"

There were nuts and oranges (that smell — why did it always sadden me?) and dancing with the rugs rolled back. Mr. Dickens even grabbed me from the corner where I was looking on and gave me a whirl, much to my embarrassment, for I had never danced a step in my life. Then he seized Cook and dragged her forward, saying, "The King must be obeyed," dancing her up and down the line while everyone clapped and shouted, "See how the King dances!"

Mirrors everywhere reflected half a hundred dancers, a dozen Christmas trees. Miss Georgy was there, of course, wearing a new dress of midnight blue silk. She was thirteen now, and quite the young lady. I stayed as far away from her as possible since I didn't want her to spoil my happiness.

Charley had been allowed to stay up much later than usual and was over-excited. He insisted on all his presents being piled in bed with him and refused to settle down. Mamie and the baby were long asleep and I didn't want him to wake them, so I told him I would sit with him and sing to him if he would lie quietly and close his eyes.

I began with my mother's favourite, "The Lark in the Clear Air": "Dear thoughts are in my mind, and my heart fills with gladness . . ." He fell asleep almost immediately. I removed the toys, putting them by the foot of the bed so he would see them when he woke up, and I went quietly to my room next door.

I could hear faint sounds of the piano as the merrymaking continued below, and I thought how glad I was that I was in service in a home where there was laughter and gaiety. I had met a few other servant girls by then, when I took Charley to the gardens in Russell Square, and I began to realize what pinched and horrible lives some of them led. Never a kind word, nothing but commands and criticism. Miss Georgy's gibes were just flea bites compared to what some of the domestic servants had to put up with. If they broke anything, it was taken out of their wages. (I thought of the teacup I had thrown against the wall. Cook said that it was Spode and part of a set.)

No affectionate words except, sometimes, the Master's . . .
"You don't know how lucky you are."

Oh I did, I did, and that night I thanked God for watching over me and prayed that I might stay with this family forever. But that was not to be.

The house in Devonshire Terrace was a long way from the hustle and bustle of my old haunts on my half-days — we had moved up in the world — but there were compensations. When the afternoons were fine, I took Charley, and sometimes Mamie, for walks in the park and visits to the zoo. Charley loved the zoo, loved feeding the bears by sticking buns on long poles. All London was fascinated by anything exotic — all London except Cook, that is, who was afraid of the lion getting loose and subjecting her to a "'orrible hend." One small ape would lope over to the farthest corner of the cage and turn his back whenever the keeper gave him a banana. I could not help but think of my feelings when being stared at while I ate. Strange — was it possible that this creature from the jungle could feel the same revulsion?

Mr. Dickens was working on a new book and bought a raven named Grip because he wanted to study ravens. It was a huge bird, lived most of the time in the stables and was learning to talk. None of us liked the bird, nor liked it when he was brought inside in his cage. Mr. Dickens said that ravens were the most intelligent birds on earth and he intended to immortalize Grip in the book he was writing.

"Isn't that so, Grip?" he would say, and the bird tipped his head to one side and looked wise.

"Say, 'Yes, Master,' Grip. Say 'Master.'" But for a long time the bird was silent.

"Useless bird," said the groom, who actually was the one in charge of it. "Now a few 'oming pigeons, *that* would be hinteresting. But no, 'e wants a raven."

Dinners were more elaborate now and Cook complained of all the washing-up, even with the help of the little scullery maid who had joined the household. The truth was that Cook didn't like to share her kitchen with anyone and had a tendency to roar at Daisy, which made her drop things, or cry, or both. I tried to be kind to her — she was just a child — but I was very busy now with the children. Mr. and Mrs. Dickens went on an extended tour of Scotland, where he was a great success in Edinburgh, and they had a terrifying journey to the Highlands. Mrs. Dickens told me she visited the house where she had been born, in Edinburgh, and she felt quite strange to think how fast time flowed. They were gone for nearly a month, and they praised us all for the way we managed the household in their absence. Only Charley seemed to resent this separation; he turned his head away when his mother went to embrace him.

(I did not tell the mistress that Miss Georgy — whose nose was out of joint, I think, for she had wanted to go to Scotland too — had dropped in several times to make sure there was no riotous living or selling of the plate going on.)

Mr. Dickens told Charley and Mamie about the Loch Ness Monster, and they both had screaming nightmares.

Grip said his first word — "cheese" — an item of which he was particularly fond. Whenever he was let loose in the garden, if you gave him a piece of cheese first, he would bury it, looking around slyly to make sure no one was watching, then waddle up and demand another.

I was now reading *Vanity Fair*, by Mr. Thackeray, but I didn't really like it. Becky Sharp was a little too sharp for my taste. I was surprised to find I did have "taste" after all.

Walter was born in February of the following year, a fine boy. Mr. Dickens called him "Young Skull" because he had no hair when he was born. Mamie was "Mild Gloster," and Katie was "Lucifer Box" because she had a temper.

"Can you cope with this menagerie, Hattie?" Mr. Dickens asked me one day. "Isn't this more than you bargained for? I sometimes think it's more than I bargained for."

"They are good children, sir."

And they were — most of the time. They adored their father but were very much in awe of him. They screamed and yelled and ran about only in the park or at the seaside. Father could be noisy at night with his parties and songs and dances, Father could roar, but that was different. However, he sang silly songs to them before they went to bed, heard their prayers and listened solemnly to their little tales of triumph or woe.

They had fun with him in a way they never did with their mother. She always seemed to be tired or fussing with a new baby. She loved them just as much — anybody could see that — but she was quiet by nature and a little inclined to melancholy. She told me once she had been unable to nurse Charley herself and felt that might have created a barrier between them. "And he grows up so fast, Hattie. They all grow up so fast."

It was decided that the stables needed painting, so Grip in his cage became a temporary resident of the parlour, for fear that he might peck at the paint and die.

"Cheese," he said, whenever anyone appeared, and one day something that sounded remotely like "Charles," which delighted both father and son.

"I told you he was an intelligent bird. Say 'Master,' Grip. Say, 'Yes, Master.'"

While Grip was in residence, it was the job of little Daisy to clean his cage every morning. She was terrified of him and always wore her bonnet, in case he tried to sit on her head. I think Grip understood that she was afraid and played up because of it; she had a terrible time getting him to return to his cage, no matter how much she tempted him with bits of bread and cheese, which she held out on a toasting fork, the way Charley fed the bears. Other than Mr. Dickens and Charley, Miss Georgina seemed to be the only one who really liked the raven. When she came to visit, she would whisper to him and he would tip his head, as though they were conspirators.

"I will be glad when the stables are finished," Mrs. Dickens said, "and that bird can go back where he belongs."

"A bird in the 'ouse," said Cook, "means a death in the 'ouse." This frightened little Daisy so much that she had a kind of fit and had to be revived with brandy and water.

"I think that's when a bird flies in," I corrected, soothing Daisy. "This bird was brought in. That's a different sort of thing altogether."

About a week later I was in the parlour, looking for Charley's spinning top, which he had mislaid the day before and now insisted on finding before he would go out.

"Hello," said Grip. I was quite startled; I hadn't realized he could say hello.

"Hello," he said, and then, as plain as plain, "Tattycoram."

"Hello Tattycoram. Hello Tattycoram. Hello, Hello."

He screeched the horrible name at the top of his voice, over and over. I couldn't bear it and searched for a cloth to cover his cage. I saw nothing big enough except a silk shawl on the piano.

I took that and threw it over the cage, but in my haste I was clumsy, and I knocked over the stand. Since I had left the parlour door open, thinking I would only be a minute, the bird flew out and down the hall shrieking "Awwk, Awwk, Awwk," as though he were about to be murdered.

Everyone came running, including Mr. Dickens.

"What the devil's going on? Harriet, what *is* the matter?"

"The cage fell over, sir, and the bird escaped. I'm sorry, sir."

"Grip," he called, "come here."

Grip ignored him, flying up and down the hall, just out of our reach. It was Cook who finally captured him with her big apron and a bit of cake.

Mr. Dickens righted the cage and placed the bird inside.

"Dear God," he said, "am I never to have any peace in this house? Bad bird," he said to Grip, then, "What is this shawl doing on the floor?"

"Pardon me, sir, I was the one who knocked the cage over. I was trying to make him stop and I grabbed the shawl and threw it over the cage and . . ." To my horror I began to sob.

"Harriet," he said, "Hattie. There's no real harm done, girl. But why did you think you had to shut him up? I can't hear him with the parlour door closed; he can squawk to his heart's content. Was this an excess of zeal on your part? If so, it has had the opposite effect, since the entire household has now been disturbed."

I continued to sob, unable to speak; but then Grip spoke for me: "Tattycoram," he said, "Hello Tattycoram, Tattycoram, Tattycoram."

Mr. Dickens quizzed every member of the household, including the groom, who had the most to do with the bird. All swore they had nothing to do with Grip's new achievement.

"Well, someone did it, and it's a very mean trick to play on Hattie. I wouldn't blame her if she gave in her notice tomorrow. And I don't care if the paint is dry or not — that bird goes back to the stables."

I was sure I knew who the culprit was. Whoever called me Coram except Miss Georgy, and who was clever enough to connect my tatting, which I always carried with me, with my name? She must have been told about the incident, for if she met me on the stairs or in the hall she gave me a sly little smile; she knew I would never accuse her, Mr. Dickens's pet. However, from that day on, she never called me Coram again.

How I hated my name, for it would always and forever be my name, even when I was an old lady — "Orfink, orfink, we know who you are, oh yes." Even the birds would say it: Tattycoram.

7

There began to be talk of America. A large map appeared on the nursery wall. Mrs. Dickens was to go, although at first she wouldn't hear of it; the baby was only nine months old. I don't know how he brought her round, but he could bring anybody round, I think, if he put his mind to it. Or maybe he just wore her down.

The Macreadys were to be left in charge of the children, although they would live in a separate house with Fred, in Osnaburgh Street. All the rest of us were to be transferred over there as well, except Mrs. Dickens's maid, Anne, who was going with them. The house in Devonshire Terrace was to be shut up until the return. When I heard that Georgina was coming to stay, to help look after the children, I was uncomfortable. I felt, perhaps wrongly, that she would do everything in her power to make my life miserable. Could I stand it for six months?

Then rescue came in a terrible way. My father sent a message that Mother was very ill, and could I possibly come home for a while to help care for her? Would Mr. Dickens release me, at least temporarily? I went that afternoon to seek him out. He was in the parlour with Mrs. Dickens, looking through a pile of books about America, so I was able to address them both at once.

"Oh, Hattie," Mrs. Dickens said, "just when we are going to need you most! Must you really go?"

But he said, "Of course she must go. Her mother will recover, and then Hattie will return to us."

"Please, sir," I said, "I think I should leave your service, for I cannot say when I'll be back."

"Leave forever?"

"Yes, sir. I'm sorry, sir."

"Are you perhaps worried about the responsibility we are thrusting upon you? The Macreadys will be just over the way, and we intend to hire another nursery maid, you know, to share the burden."

"I am not afraid of responsibility, but it may well be that my mother's illness will be a lengthy one. I suspect she is very ill or she never would have allowed my father to ask this, never. I don't want to have divided loyalties."

"Well, well," he said, after a moment, "this is news indeed, and it comes at a bad time. However, your mother didn't choose to fall ill, and if you feel your place is with her, you must go. The children will miss you terribly; we shall all miss you terribly."

Mrs. Dickens looked so woebegone I felt pulled in two. She had been counting on me, I could see that, and yet, kind soul that she was, she never said another word of reprimand. Instead, she told me she would inform Fred and Miss Georgy that if I should want to return to London, I was to be welcomed back.

On the first of January, a hazy, frosty morning, I left directly after breakfast. Mr. and Mrs. Dickens and her maid were to depart the following day. Mr. Dickens thought it would be best to have the leave-takings more or less all at once, and I was not to tell the children I would probably not return.

"For of course you *shall* be back. I feel it in my bones."

But Charley sensed something, and he clung sobbing to my skirts and would not be comforted. He created a great wet patch where the tears ran down. Mrs. Dickens gave me a pair of garnet eardrops and some ivory threaders for my tatting; Mr. Dickens gave me a purse of money — "to be used toward making your mother comfortable" — and Cook showed her affection through an enormous parcel of food. Fred shook hands, Mamie and Katie kissed me, and even the baby was held up for a kiss.

Mr. Dickens went with me in a cab as far as the Queen of Sheba, where I was to board the coach. The horses' manes and ears were tipped with frost. He said he would soon enough be on board a ship, unable to take his daily constitutional, and so he would enjoy the walk back. It was a bitterly cold day, and I suspected he was just being kind.

"I hope you will think well of the menagerie when you are back home."

"Yes, sir. Of course I shall."

He hated goodbyes — even the children never said goodbye to him — so I was not surprised when he thrust a small parcel into my hands, then turned and walked rapidly away.

He had paid for me to have an inside seat as far as Guildford, where my father had arranged for a wagon to meet the coach, so as soon as I was settled, I opened the package. There was a copy of his very first book, *The Pickwick Papers*, signed by him on the flyleaf: "To Miss Harriet Coram, with affection, Charles Dickens." And underneath, "Two and twenty. Two and twenty. Two and twenty." It was the first time had had ever given me one of his own books, although I now had a small library of other works he had presented to me. There was also, tucked in the pages and folded to fit, a drawing by Charley of myself and the children visiting the hippopotamus at the zoo. Charley is drawn much larger than his sisters and the baby, and I am not much bigger.

I'm afraid the London streets went by in a blur of tears.

My mother greeted me with her usual smile and outstretched arms, but she was lying on a bed before the fire. Although she sat up when I came in, she did not stand. I was shocked by the change in her; she had lost a great deal of weight and her eyes looked huge in her thin face.

Father made the tea, something I had never seen him do before, and I put out some slices of the fruitcake Cook had sent. I could not help but notice Mother only crumbled hers, to make me think she was eating. When she sent Father off to the White Horse to get some rum for a toddy — "just to take the chill off your journey, Hattie" — she lifted up her nightdress and showed me her belly; it was as swollen as though she were with child.

"Are you in pain, Mother?"

"Not so much in pain as uncomfortable. My insides are all stopped up."

"Has the doctor come? I have money . . ."

"My dear child, the doctor has come several times, and the Misses Bray have paid, bless their kind hearts."

"Is there nothing —?"

"There's an operation, but Hattie, I don't think I could bear it. It's silly, but I don't want to be cut open. I have a horror of it."

"Oh, Mam, not even to save your life?"

"Not even for that. Whatever happens now is God's will."

"How can you say that? Why would God want you to

suffer? Why would there *be* an operation if that weren't God's will?"

"No, no, don't get yourself upset, I've made my decision. Father and I have discussed it, and we are both reconciled to it."

"Well, I am not reconciled to it. Mother, please, I don't want to lose you. I can't bear to lose you."

I was sitting on the bed, holding her hand (her thin hand), and now I began to weep.

"Hattie, stop this now. You must be strong and help your father to be strong. I want no more tears. Only smiles."

The temperature dropped even further that night, and through the small window in the bedroom I looked up at the pale, cold, indifferent moon. How cruel life was. How cruel the Creator. He gave me a second mother, a good mother, and now He was going to take her away. What was the point of it all? Why were we here?

I, who had been so lovingly looked after by this woman and this man, took over the management of the house, and when February came my father went back to work in the fields. I could see that both of them were relieved to have him out of the house, for he was a man who couldn't bear to be idle; his misery and frustration at Mother's illness brought us all low. They had never slept apart since their wedding day, but now she insisted that he go upstairs at night (he had made a partition and turned the one room into two), and she would call out to us if she needed anything. I think sometimes our energy and our constant efforts to tempt her to eat or to make her more comfortable exhausted her.

My mother was very popular, and many of the village women came to call. They brought food as well as gossip, and my mother always seemed cheered, if tired, after these visits. Many commented with approval on the fact that I had returned from the city to nurse my foster mother. The Misses Bray visited as well, always bringing some delicacy — an egg custard, blackberry cordial, even hothouse grapes. They told me privately that they had done everything possible to persuade my mother to undergo the operation — she could have the best specialist in the country — but she would not be moved.

"And we must tell you, my dear, that the doctor said the operation itself carries great risks and is often unsuccessful. There is not too much hope for this sort of thing."

In the evenings Father smoked his pipe — Mother said the smell of tobacco gave her comfort — and I told them about Charley and Mamie and Katie and the baby, about Fred and Cook. I told them of how Mr. and Mrs. Dickens were in America, and that Mrs. Dickens had not wanted to leave her children but he got round her by saying he needed her more than the children did, talked about what grand times they would have in Boston and New York, impressed upon her his observation that small children had no sense of time anyway.

"Perhaps he is right about very small children," I said, "but I think Charley will be counting the days."

"How could she leave her children — for how long, did you say?"

"Six months at the very least."

"Six months! I could never leave my children for six months. And to be separated by an ocean . . ." I knew she was thinking of Sam.

"Ah," I said, "but you are not married to Mr. Charles Dickens — he always gets his own way. And to tell the truth, I think he was nervous about going alone, although he would never admit it. And her maid has gone as well."

"Her maid as well!" It was all too much for her.

Mother hung on, all through the spring, which was particularly lovely that year. We placed her bed so that she could feel the warmth come in through the open door. Father brought her posies of wildflowers — primroses, bluebells, whatever was bright and fresh and full of promise; she smiled at him and touched his cheek with her finger. "Remember how you used to bring me flowers when we were courting? And you were so shy and nervous, they were nearly dead from the sweat of your hand by the time you presented them."

"You were the only lass for me," he said, his voice thick. "There was never anyone else."

"Not even Beatie Chapman?" she said, and to me, "Beatie was the prettiest girl in the village, always Queen of the May."

"Beatie Chapman was a little minx," he said. "Beatie Chapman was not a girl to spend your life with."

"Where is she now?" I asked, enjoying this moment of smiles and intimacy between the two of them.

"Ah, she married a lad from Dorking, a fellow she met at the fair. Nobody's seen much of her since. Her parents are long dead, but I don't remember many visits when they were still alive."

"No," repeated my father, "Beatie was not a girl to spend your life with, not a girl to marry."

My days were busy with household duties, and, if Mother were comfortable, I often went for long walks on the Downs in the afternoons, or I sat by the Tillingbourne and watched the children playing the same game with twig boats that Jonnie and I had played. I thought of the dead girl I had called a princess and the stories the village gossips put about concerning her: she was with child. Stories I didn't understand at the time. Some said it was her oldest brother.

I picked cowslips, for cowslip wine, and elderberries. Mushrooms. Later, in the autumn, hazelnuts, which I dried before the fire. I picked blindly and without pleasure, knowing Mother would be gone before the next year rolled around. I picked an enormous basket of hurts and made pies, something nice to offer the village women when they called. I even enticed Mother into eating little sups of hurt preserves off a spoon.

The doctor came once a week now and left opiates, which she took with sips of water. And still she lingered on, through harvest time, through the coming of winter. As the pains grew worse, I gave her more and more laudanum, so that she spent her last few days in a kind of dream and did not speak. But before that, in the last week, she whispered to me, "You are a good girl, Hattie, the best daughter I could have wished for. And I'll tell you a secret — I loved you best of all the hospital children."

She died on Christmas Day. The bells began to ring for church just as she drew her final breaths. I think she imagined she was already dead and the bells were ringing for her as she entered God's kingdom.

"Lovely," she whispered, "lovely." And then she died.

For a long time we couldn't move, just sat there holding her cold hands. Then Father closed her eyes and went to get the women for the laying out. I wanted to do it, but he said that was not the custom and her friends would be offended, that as soon as I could face it, I should go along to the church and tell the rector that she was dead.

"I don't want to leave her alone!"

"All right, lass, wait here until I come back."

Except for the princess (and she didn't really count), I had never seen a dead person before. Children had died at the Foundling, of course, and were given nice funerals, but their caskets were closed. When I looked at my mother's corpse, I felt as though I were looking at a stranger, for when her spirit left, she left too. I was not overwhelmed by grief — that would come later, along with the panic, the feeling of abandonment. I was simply relieved that her terrible suffering was over.

She was certain that she would be reunited with her parents in Heaven and with her nine dead babies, as well as with Sam and Jonnie, if they were no longer alive. I wasn't sure what I thought about heavenly reunions, perhaps because I was afraid I would meet the woman who had given me up or even the man who was my father. I realized I no longer wished for any such meeting, on Earth or in Heaven.

That evening, as the bells tolled for my mother's death, I wrote to Mr. Brownlow to inform him and to request, if it were possible, the names and addresses of the other eight children she had fostered over the years. Some of them might wish to come to her funeral. He replied almost at once, saying it was against hospital policy for me to have the names and addresses, but he would write himself to the ones whose addresses were still known. Could I please let him know when the funeral was to be? He praised my mother and went on to say that all her foster children had returned to the hospital sound in body and mind and that I must be very proud of her and honour her memory.

I don't know if he was unable to reach the other orphans in time, but none of them appeared or so much as sent a note. This made me angry, it seemed so ungrateful, but perhaps they had all moved away. Once girls were twenty-one, or boys twenty-four, we were no longer wards of the hospital and were free to do whatever we liked with our lives. And the funeral was lovely, even without those others. The entire village came, and the hospital sent a wreath of white roses and ivy to lay on top of the casket. The church was decorated with holly and swags of pine, and the Misses Bray had provided two enormous pillar candles of beeswax for the altar. The smell of pine and honey filled the little church. Afterwards, they hosted a lunch at the White Horse Inn for all who wished to come. My father sat at the head of one of the long tables, but like a sleepwalker, he hardly seemed to know where he was. Snow fell silently outside, and we walked home hand in hand through the muffled world. Soon it was the New Year, and it seemed impossible that we could go on without her.

My father seemed suddenly bent and old, although he was not much past fifty. He almost never spoke unless I addressed him first. In truth, he did not have enough to occupy him, and so he brooded. I think, if he had not considered it a sin, he would have joined Mother.

I began to read to him, of an evening, from *Robinson Crusoe,* and this cheered him a bit. He found it admirable the way Crusoe managed to make a life for himself on that desolate island. I told him Mr. Dickens said the story was based on a real man and a real shipwreck.

"You don't say so — a real man?"

"Yes, Father, and he really did all those things."

"Oh my! And that black fellow, Friday, was he there too?

"I don't know about Friday. I think so."

He sighed. "I feel like that — shipwrecked — since she

went. But perhaps you are my Man Friday, Hattie, here to keep me company?"

"I won't leave, Father, you do know that? I won't ever leave you."

He leaned across to my chair and grasped my hand.

"I must tell you something, Hattie, that I never told her, never let on to anyone. When she first started this fostering business — she'd heard about it from a cousin over to Farnham — I didn't like the idea, I didn't like it at all. But when her first two babies died, and she was so low, I thought I should reconcile myself to the idea. Then Sam came, but she was used to it by then, and I got used to it as well — sometimes she had two babies at once! — and so she kept on. Just as well, because her own babies kept dying, poor things. But I never really liked those babies the way she did. Until you. Mebbe it was because of Jonnie, because he lived, even though the little girl died, but suddenly it all made sense, that she wanted to help raise a strange woman's child, that she would put it to the breast. And you were such a lively little thing and so fond of us all . . . well, I just wanted you to know all this. I was as fond of you myself as if you were my own. And now — look at the blessing you have been. There are many natural daughters who would not have done as much as you. God works in mysterious ways, He truly does."

I could say nothing in reply, just hold onto his hand and sob.

And later, when I came across a small packet of letters from the hospital, I found in one a lock of my hair, "as requested." So it hadn't been for my first mother after all.

8

In the summer of 1843 the Misses Bray came to see me. They wished to set up a proper school in the village; would I be interested in teaching there?

"But I have never taught anyone."

"Harriet, you can read, and you write a good hand, as we saw in the note you sent us after your mother's funeral. The rector vouches for you, and the need for education in this village is great. You are as yet unmarried and without the encumbrance of children at home. All that we would require is basic reading and writing, simple arithmetic, handicrafts for the girls and some religious instruction."

"I would have to ask my father."

"Lass," he said, "it's a good thing. It would provide you with a bit of money and keep you by me at the same time."

"I've told you, Father, I won't leave you, money or no money."

"Do you not think of returning to London some day?"

"Not really. I like it here with you."

This was not strictly true. I did like it in the village and I would never leave my father, but I sometimes felt very lonely. Most of the women my age were long married and had children. They greeted me warmly, but I could see that they didn't feel we had much in common. Even my accent was different. I missed my walks through the busy streets — so much to look at and listen to. I felt old before my time, and although I loved my father, I knew that some day he would be gone and I would be all alone, with no one to cook for or care for. It was almost comical: on the one hand, I was a bastard, some unknown couple's child and, in the world's eyes, a nothing, a naught; on the other, my life in the Dickens household, where both my speech and manners had been polished and my love of reading encouraged — these things set me apart from the villagers in quite the opposite way.

The new curate came to call, a limp young man who fancied himself, and although I gave him tea and he praised my scones, I made no effort to attract his interest. I was sure someone appropriate would soon snatch him up, perhaps one of the young ladies from the big houses in the parish. As for myself, I could never be happy with such an earnest, joyless creature. I had a feeling his face might break if he laughed, and he constantly patted his lips with a white handkerchief.

What were my prospects if I stayed? Nursery maid to one of the rich families? Maybe even parlour maid, with ribbons in my cap? A word from Mr. and Mrs. Charles Dickens would assure me of good employment in that line. I decided being a teacher was vastly preferable to that, and so I told the Misses Bray I would be pleased to try it, and try it I did.

For four years I taught at that little school, and I did become quite good at it, expanding the syllabus to include geography, because I was interested in that subject. The Misses Bray bought a large map of the world, with all the Empire marked in pink. It hung on the wall behind my desk, next to a picture of the Queen and Prince Albert in their best clothes. It amazed the children to think that there could be such places as Africa or

South America. They knew about Australia, if only to hear of, because that's where the convicts went.

They wrote on their slates:

The North Wind doth blow
And we shall have Snow
And what will the Robin do then
Poor thing?

The size of my class depended on the season, for at sowing time and harvest time the older children disappeared to work in the fields alongside their parents. And if a new baby was born, an older sister might have to stop at home for a few weeks.

We burned peat in an iron stove, and I shall forever associate that sweet, acrid, eye-watering smell with the squeak of chalk on slates and the sound of children's voices, more or less in unison, reciting the four times table.

And now, for the first time, I felt part of the community. I was "the schoolmistress"; I was "the teacher"; I had a clearly defined role. I went to church with Father every Sunday, never failing to say a prayer in the churchyard, where Mother lay beside her parents and her children. I helped at the village fetes, where my tatting and fancywork were very much admired by the gentry. My pies were applauded at the harvest dinners.

In the years since my return, I had continued my habit of long walks; sometimes Father went with me, but from spring until past harvest time he was usually too busy and seldom came home before dusk. I often thought of the day I left the Foundling, when Mr. Dickens had said to me, "Do you like to walk, Harriet?" and my pert reply. I'm surprised he didn't turn me around right then and march me back inside.

I continued my rambles and brought back things for the

children to examine: an abandoned robin's nest, the shed skin of a grass snake, a razor-sharp fungus from the Hurtwood. One day a boy brought in a dead crow, and we admired the glossy blackness of its feathers and the lightness of its bones.

"Why can't we fly, Miss?"

"Because we are too heavy, and besides, we have no wings."

"Angels have wings, Miss. We'll all have wings one day."

No one called me "orfink" or "fondling." It was "Good morning, Miss Coram," "Good afternoon, Miss Coram," "Yes, Miss," "No, Miss," "Please, Miss, I know the answer, Miss."

The curate married a pale girl from Albury; she had very little chin and seemed almost as limp as he was. In time, I thought, they will produce a string of pale, boneless children — and told myself not to be so nasty.

Then my father died, suddenly, just keeled over while he was walking behind a plough. No time to make our farewells, no time for me to tell him once again how much I loved him.

There was his pipe on the mantel, his clean smock-frock drying on the line. I had never been so alone before and could not adjust to it. The little cottage was full of ghosts, and although I tried to tire myself out with teaching and walking, I slept badly and had terrible dreams. Sometimes I was back at the Foundling and had been thrust into a ring of fine ladies, all pointing their fingers and chanting "base-born! base-born!" or a stern voice was commanding, "Hold out your hands!" Sometimes I was on a London street in the fog and night creatures were clutching at my skirts. I went down street after street, trying to find my way home. Street after street, turning this way and that, but nothing looked familiar. Once I dreamed I was being walled up like the anchorite and woke up screaming.

There were several nights after his passing when, sleepless, I sat downstairs, wrapped in an old shawl of my mother's, and never went up to my bedroom at all.

And there were practical things to worry about. We did not own the cottage of course (somehow I had forgotten that when imagining my future), and I knew I would have to leave, perhaps right away. Would I end up a domestic servant after all? I seemed sunk in a bog of grief and worry; it was all I could do to drag myself to school each morning. When I helped to arrange the flowers in the church, I looked towards the place where Christine, the anchorite, had had herself walled up. Twice! She came out and then she went back in. How could anyone do that? Was she allowed to speak to the person who delivered her daily bread and water, or had she taken a vow of silence as well? There were stories in the village, passed down from generation to generation, that after she died and her body was brought out, her fingers were worn down past the first joint, that there were gouges in the wall where she had tried to remove some bricks. If that were so, then there was more to the story than we thought. What if she had not gone willingly? What if it were punishment, not devotion, that placed her there? Was she one of the unwise virgins perhaps? Was she taken in adultery?

Whatever was to become of me, even if it meant cleaning out grates at dawn and carrying cans of water up and down stairs, even if it meant encountering another Miss Georgina (and I had heard that some of the farmers' daughters were just as high-handed with their servants), I would never be walled up again for any reason; I would never give up on life. I had had enough of walls and silence at the Foundling.

Once again, my benefactors came to my rescue. The Misses Bray had decided to buy our cottage from the farmer who owned it, but he balked at this, said it was a labourer's cottage and a labourer's cottage it would remain. However, if they were willing to pay the rents, I could remain until the next Lady Day.

"And before that," said Miss Amelia, "we shall have built a teacherage."

"We need a teacherage anyway," said Miss Louisa.

"You must let me pay the rents."

"Nonsense, my dear. Your stipend is so low, we couldn't allow it."

"Is there no way I can repay you for your kindness?"

Miss Amelia smiled. "The daughter of a young cousin is getting married. We have seen examples of your embroidery and tatting, and we wondered, if we brought over a set of linen — sheets and pillowcases — if you could embroider something on them and do a pretty edge?"

"I would be pleased to do that."

That night I thought of something my father had said when I was reading to him from *Robinson Crusoe*: "Wonderful, the way he got on. No lyin' down and given' up for that one, Hattie, none o' that."

Here I had been bemoaning my lot like some spoiled, incompetent girl. I did not deserve the Misses Bray. There were no Misses Bray to haul Robinson Crusoe out of his despair, no Misses Bray to say, "We'll build you a house, my dear."

The teaching continued; the children came and went. Thanks to the rector, I was able to get some music sent out from London and I even began part-singing with them. I thought we might give a little concert on May Day.

Now is the month of May-ing
With lads and lasses play-ing
Fa la la la la, fa la la la la
Fa la la la la — lah.

I adopted a little black kitten — or the kitten adopted me — and I found myself confiding in him as though he could understand. I let him sleep in my bed, and his small contented hum seemed to take the edge off my loneliness at night. Soon he began to present me with gifts of mice and voles, and I decided to name him Orion after the mighty hunter in the sky, Ori for short.

And then, one morning, a "Whoa!" and a great clatter of hooves outside the schoolroom door. The children dropped everything and jostled for space at the windows to see who had come to visit us. I thought it might be the bishop and looked anxiously around to see if everything was in order.

It was Mr. Dickens, dismounting from a big black horse.

"Give them a half-holiday," he commanded. "I must talk to you."

"I can't do that, sir."

"Of course you can. You're in charge here, aren't you?"

"We are in the midst of a lesson."

"Yes, well, lessons can wait. What are you in the midst of?"

"Simple fractions, sir."

"Well, one-half plus one-third is still going to make five-sixths tomorrow, isn't it? That's not going to change."

He turned to a boy named Noel.

"You, boy. What's one-half of sixteen?"

"Eight, sir."

"Very good. Here's a sixpence."

Then such a show of hands! "Try me, sir! Try me!"

He smiled at me in his old pleased-with-myself way, but I was not pleased.

"I can meet you at the end of school, sir, and not before."

"And what am I to do while I'm waiting?"

"There's an excellent inn here, the White Horse, on the west side of Shere Lane. Just carry on past the stream towards the square, and you will come to it."

"Is there a stable in the village?"

"Of course."

"Very well, although why I should give in to you I don't know. I've half a mind to go away again and not tell you why I've come."

"As you wish, sir."

"Heighty-teighty. But all right, I shall meet you outside the White Horse at — at what time?"

"At half past two."

He mounted his horse and clattered away down the lane.

"Who was that, Miss?"

"Was that your sweetheart, Miss?"

"Was that your long-lost brother?"

Great envy fell upon Noel and his sixpence, which I feared might be taken from him before the day was out. Several boys were much bigger than he was.

"That," I said, "is the greatest writer in England, and if you are very good and finish this lesson, perhaps I shall read you a story."

They were good and did reasonably well at their lessons, and so after dinner I took out *Oliver Twist*. I did not begin at the beginning, but commenced at Chapter Two: "For the next eight or ten months, Oliver was the victim of a systematic course of treachery and deception — he was brought up by hand."

By the time I met him at the inn, Mr. Dickens seemed to be on a first-name basis with all the old men in the village. He could speak with authority about the Tillingbourne or the Hurtwood or the possible price of wheat this coming harvest. Even his accent had been modified to sound more countrified; I knew he was acting a part and enjoying it. He said he had never before in his lifetime partaken of such an excellent steak and kidney pudding and would have to bring his best friends down from London to dine at the inn. He reckoned there wasn't a prettier village or a finer inn to be found in all southwest England.

"Shall we go to your home?" he asked me.

I did not think it would be proper, since I was living alone, so I suggested we sit at one of the big tables the landlord had set out under the trees. He asked if I would take anything and I accepted a ginger beer.

"I expect teaching is thirsty work."

"Yes, it is."

"But rewarding."

"Most of the time."

"Tell me about it, Harriet."

And so I told him about my scholars, particularly the naughty ones, for I knew that would please him. Of Noel, who always had to be first and wanted to be a sailor when he grew up. Of James, a shy boy who wrote his name on everything as if to convince himself that he really did exist. Of the girls and their skipping games and their ever-changing best friends.

"I see you smile, I see your face light up, and I think perhaps I have come in vain."

"I do not wish to go into service again, sir, not if I can avoid it."

"You did not enjoy your time with us?"

"That's not the point. I would not enjoy being in service to the Queen of England."

"I shall tell her that, the next time I see her." (But I knew he was only joking.) "Now listen to me for a moment, Harriet, and don't interrupt until I finish. Agreed?"

I nodded but had made up my mind not to be taken in by him.

"There is a wealthy lady in London called Miss Burdett-Coutts. You may have heard me mention her, for she is Charley's godmother and always sends the Twelfth Night cake. However, she is much more than that."

I frowned. I thought I could see what was coming.

"A frown like that is an interruption, Harriet, but I shall not stop to inquire why you frown at the mention of this generous and kind-hearted lady. In any event, she and I — her money, my ability to organize things — are going to open a home for destitute women, or fallen women, if you will, in Shepherd's Bush. We have leased the building and grounds, the furnishing and decorating are going ahead at a great rate, and in a few months we shall be open for business."

He leaned across the table, his brown eyes sparkling with excitement.

"You see, Harriet, I have a theory — and Miss Burdett-Coutts agrees with me — that some of these poor women, most of whom are in prison at the moment, for I think we shall draw exclusively from the prisons, at least to begin with — that some of these poor women should be given a second chance. Given such a chance, and instructed in good moral habits as well as good housekeeping, they would be excellent candidates for emigration to Australia, or even to America."

"I don't see what this has to do with me."

"Let me finish. I have engaged a matron, an excellent woman named Mrs. Morton, but I would like her to have at least one assistant, someone with a good head on her shoulders, someone who, because of her own background, perhaps might feel some sympathy for these woman. I observed you, Harriet, during your years with us. I think you are both sensible and spirited, and I know you have a kind heart. I thought of you immediately, and I told Miss Burdett-Coutts I would come down here personally to see if I could interest you in the situation. You would live in and all your meals would be included, as well as tea and sugar and an allowance for suitable clothing. I would not want you to wear anything resembling a uniform, just simple, attractive dress and sensible footwear. You will have your own room and share a private sitting room with Matron. There will also be generous free time and a salary of ten pounds a quarter. What do you think?"

He sat back and waited for me to say yes.

This home — was it not just another kind of prison? What if the women didn't want to be saved? And there would be strict rules and regulations; I knew Mr. Dickens well enough to take that as a given. Didn't he run his own household in a rather military fashion? But it would be Matron and myself who would ultimately be responsible for seeing that these sows' ears were transformed into silk purses. What if we failed?

Finally I said, "I don't know."

"What don't you know?"

"I don't know if I am the right person for this."

"And I know you are; I'm sure of it. I shall be very involved myself — this is a project dear to my heart. I intend to be concerned with every aspect of the business."

"May I think about it?"

"For how long? I'm impatient to get this settled."

"A few days?"

"How many?" He leaned forward again. "Harriet, wouldn't you like to do something for these poor souls? We are going to take in only those we feel are worthy, those who would benefit from a second chance."

I suppose the words "second chance" set me off.

"Just as my first mother got a second chance." How bitterly I said it. "By abandoning me, she could pretend 'all that' — meaning me, her infant daughter — never happened. She didn't need to emigrate. All she had to do was convince the Governors she was a creature of good character and then walk away from me forever."

"Is that how you see it? I'm surprised, truly I am. She did not, in fact, abandon you. She took you to a place where she knew you would be cared for. Would you have preferred that the two of you starved to death in the workhouse? And these women I am talking about are not 'fallen' in the same sense. They are women who have turned to prostitution or theft in order to keep body and soul together. None of them have children, abandoned or otherwise."

"So far as you know."

"Agreed. So far as we know."

I had been tracing patterns on the tabletop with my finger. Now I raised my eyes to his, and I could see that he was taken aback by my lack of gratitude.

"It's difficult to explain," I said. "You come out of such places as the Foundling with a mark on you — invisible to others, maybe, or maybe not — which is with you the rest of your life. Perhaps it would be better to die beside our mothers in the workhouse. At least we would know they loved us.

"And then to be sent into the country, to our foster mothers, to let us live in the bosom of a family for four or five years, at which time a number is once again hung round our necks and we are snatched away to be locked up behind stone walls. If we had never known freedom, it would not have been so bad. Twice abandoned, twice! Don't talk to me about second chances."

He stood up. "I think, then, that I have your answer already."

I took a deep breath. "No. I said I would think about it, and I will."

"But if you are already prejudiced against the scheme, then you would be of no use to us. I'm sorry; I should not have come; I had no idea."

I too stood up and tried to smile.

"I don't think I had any idea myself that I felt so strongly about my history. I have never spoken out like that before. In truth, I am very fortunate, and in my heart I hope my first mother did get her second chance and is thriving somewhere."

"I hope so too."

He called for his horse to be brought round from the stables, and we waited a few minutes in silence. The air was so still, I could hear men calling to their horses far away in the fields.

"You haven't asked after Mrs. Dickens and the children."

"Are they well?"

"Charley is ten now, a real little man. I have put him down for Eton. The girls are a delight, the baby no longer resembles a plump and tasty turkey but resembles himself, and himself is rather naughty. And there are others since you left us, Francis and Alfred. One more will pop out any day. Mrs. Dickens seems to be carrying on a Malthusian experiment of her own. Sometimes I feel like Macbeth, when the witches show him the vision of Banquo's children: 'What, will the line stretch out to the crack of doom?'"

"And Fred?"

"Ah, Fred is in love — or thinks he is." (This said with a sideways look, so I did not pursue the matter.)

"Miss Georgina is with us more or less permanently now," he said. "We could not do without her." He paused. "You did not ask about Miss Georgina."

"I was thinking only of the immediate family, sir — the household as I knew it when I left."

"I think from now on you will have to include Miss Georgina as well. Unless she marries, but she swears she won't. She has already turned down one good offer. I think she is with us forever."

"And the raven?"

"Strange you should mention the raven. Grip is long dead, having eaten something that disagreed with him. After his demise, when the gardener was digging a new herbaceous border, the most amazing things turned up. Bits of mouldy cheese, of course, and string, but also a lead soldier Walter had accused Francis of eating, one of Mrs. Dickens's pearl eardrops and a golden guinea! I had him stuffed, by the way."

The horse came up, and the landlord stepped out to wish Mr. Dickens Godspeed. Just before he turned north towards Upper Street and the road to Guildford, he leaned down and beckoned to me.

"How many scholars attend your school?"

"Sixteen are enrolled. The number actually attending varies from season to season and day to day."

He pulled out his purse and handed me three half-crowns.

"Get our good landlord to change this into sixpences, will you, and distribute them tomorrow."

"Sir," I said, looking up at him (he was magnificent on that big black horse), "I'm sorry for what I said just now."

"No, no. You spoke from the heart. You may not believe it, but I have some ancient grievances buried deep in mine, and someday they too may come out. I merely hope you will give the offer some thought."

I promised I would write to him within the week and off he galloped, with small boys and barking dogs running after.

I walked down to my quiet cottage — the teacherage was not yet finished — and sat for a long time with the cat in my lap. I was shocked at the bitterness that I still felt towards that young woman who had left me at the Foundling Hospital. For the first time I wondered what her name was and whether she had given me a name, or had she simply called me Baby, knowing she would give me away? Miss Georgy had said I looked like a gypsy; I had met gypsies in the Hurtwood, with Sam and Jonnie, and many times since. I could see a slight resemblance, but my skin was much too pale. Mrs. Dickens thought Irish was closer to the truth. Besides, the gypsies looked after their own; they did not give babies away to strangers. I rocked and rocked while the dark came on, and the tears fell, and Orion hummed in my lap.

9

"Harriet," said Mr. Dickens one day, coming in with some swatches of cloth, "you hated the uniforms at the Foundling, did you not?"

"I never said so, sir."

"Hmm. I seem to recall an incident with a teacup . . ."

I could feel my cheeks burn.

"What I disliked, in that case, was the idea of using the Foundling uniform as fancy dress."

"I see, my mistake. You felt it made a mockery of the uniform."

"It wasn't a fancy dress."

"No, of course not. But I suspect you didn't like the uniforms."

"Nobody did."

"Because they seemed old-fashioned?"

"It wasn't only that. They set us apart, they marked us for what we were."

"Ah, yes, it's there in the very name; uniforms lead to uniformity. We in this country are so fond of uniforms and badges, of monotonous repetition of dull garb — especially for charitable institutions. Everybody alike, no individuality. I suppose it makes practical sense: all the cloth could be bought in quantity, no doubt at a discount. Now, Miss Burdett-Coutts has sent over some samples of cloth. Speaking frankly, I do not like the idea.

Economical uniforms may be, but deadly dull. I get depressed just looking at the cloth, and I have two thoughts on why it should be rejected: one, I do not think the residents of Urania Cottage should wear anything resembling a uniform, and two, I think they should wear dresses of various colours — not gaudy, but definitely not the colour of mud. Do you agree?"

"I do. So long as Miss Burdett-Coutts does not object on the grounds of expense."

He smiled. "Miss Burdett-Coutts always takes my direction in these matters." (I could not help but notice he was wearing one of his most outlandish waistcoats that day, a veritable meadow of colour.)

"I will send this dull drugget back immediately and order some brighter stuff. But we must hurry; I have the measurements of our first residents, and we are due to open in a fortnight. A seamstress will arrive tomorrow to help you."

At the door he turned around.

"With different colours and slight variations in design, no one should point to these women when they are out walking and identify them with Urania Cottage. And colour is so necessary to a cheerful disposition, don't you think?" He smiled at me. "By the way, Harriet, do you know who designed the uniforms for the Foundling Hospital?"

"No, sir."

"William Hogarth, the great painter. His portrait of Captain Coram hangs in the girls' dining hall."

I was silent.

"You are not impressed?"

On the point of leaving, he came back and sat down.

"There is one other thing."

"Yes, sir?"

"I am hoping you won't think I am disparaging you in any way — you must know in what high esteem I hold you — but would you consider changing your name?"

"My name?"

"Yes. For the time being. For as long as you are at Urania Cottage. I'm talking about your last name, of course — Coram."

"And why would I want to do that?"

"Two and twenty, Harriet, two and twenty! It just occurred to me that these girls might respect you less if they heard the name Coram, for of course they would know immediately that you were brought up at the Foundling."

"Would they, sir? Immediately?"

"I'm afraid so."

"I think I'll keep my name, nevertheless. Perhaps I can serve as an example to them — through my name, I mean."

"I hadn't thought of that. Yes. An example. Excellent."

I thoroughly disliked him at that moment, for it was obvious he had paid no attention to my tone of voice.

He left, satisfied, and I sat there, trembling with anger.

My sewing suffered that night; I had to unpick it all the next day and start again. I went to see Mr. Dickens and said I would change my name — to Harriet Naughton.

Shepherd's Bush was not precisely the back of beyond, but it was close. Quite rural until a few years before, it still had market gardens to feed the capital and gravel pits north of the green. At night, even in our area, it was not safe. However, the house was large and pleasant, each girl had her own room, and the experiment seemed to be off to a good start; the first girl wept when she saw her room and was handed the key to her bedroom door. Like anyone, Mr. Dickens appreciated spontaneous displays of gratitude.

As I suspected, there were a great many rules and regulations, drawn up by Mr. Dickens and approved by Miss Burdett-Coutts, but these girls, who had come straight from prison, were used to rules and regulations and accepted them without protest, at least at first. If they expected life here would be more relaxed on that score, they were very much mistaken. There was a set time to get up, a set time for bed, regular times for meals. And there was a "Marks System," which Mr. Dickens had based on the ideas of a prison reformer he knew. A thousand marks would earn a girl six shillings and sixpence, and if she received high scores in most of the categories (Temper, Punctuality, Industry, Truthfulness, and so on) she might earn as much as £2.12s a year. Each girl had her own book, which was kept in Matron's desk drawer. I think Truthfulness was the most difficult for them; since they had spent years practising falsehood and deception, the lies came automatically. And they stole — ridiculous things like a reel of cotton or a button from the button box, nothing they really needed — just for the excitement, to see what they could get away with. Sometimes they reminded me of Grip.

The first time they were caught, they were reprimanded; the second time, they were sent away. This seemed very hard to me, but Mr. Dickens said that if Urania Cottage were to succeed, its inhabitants had to accept and abide by the rules. There should be no exceptions.

The first girl who was dismissed, Nora Doyle, affected us all. A pretty Irish girl of about nineteen, she had been on the streets since childhood. She not only stole — a teaspoon, embroidery floss, a quarter pound of tea from the caddy — she cursed like a sailor. And yet there she was, down on her knees, weeping and begging for another chance. She'd be a good girl now, she promised she would, only don't send her away.

Mr. Dickens shook his head.

"This is exactly what you said the last time, Nora."

"Oh, I'm a backslider, sir, I am that. I'm a wicked girl, but I'm tryin'."

It was coming on to Christmas and dark at four in the afternoon. Matron fetched a bonnet and a warm shawl from the store cupboard, and Mr. Dickens gave her a shilling to pay for a place to spend the night.

I shall never forget the sight of that girl going out the door, her face all swollen with weeping, and Mr. Dickens turning to us with tears in his own eyes; "I had no choice." We included Nora in our evening prayers that night. God knows what happened to her. I thought I saw her once, in a doorway, but I was never sure.

My own duties were not onerous, the chief one being to teach reading, writing and handicrafts. Most of the girls could barely write their names, and so I could have been back in the little school in Shere, watching the children frown as they practised big A and little a or sounded out a word from a primer. They liked handicrafts better, and some became excellent knitters and embroiderers. They began to put away articles they could take with them to Australia or South Africa when the time came. (The possibility of marriage in a new land, with their past behind them, had been hinted at but never guaranteed.) Matron and I together instructed them in basic household duties, for it was a given that, whatever their lives might be like eventually, they would arrive on distant shores trained as domestic servants. Miss Burdett-Coutts had an arrangement with certain bishops, who would see to placing them in good homes. (I suppose she meant the homes of officers or of colonists.) They even learned to bake bread, and in the springtime, under the direction of the gardener, they planted seeds in the back garden.

They talked about the future sometimes, chattering away in the evenings, one or the other of them with Ori on her lap — like most cats, he was fond of laps. What would it be like, the long ocean voyage, the new country? Nearly all were determined to find a protector, in the form of a husband, although we tried to discourage such talk. When it turned ten o'clock and each repaired to her solitary cot, what did they dream about, I wonder.

After a year our first girls set out in twos and threes, modest in dress and manner, ready to be born again into respectability (of the servant class, of course). They travelled steerage, and we heard later about the few who had succumbed to temptation and taken up their old ways on the voyage out. I was never quite sure what happened to those few (and they were few) and didn't want to ask. They certainly wouldn't be sent back to England. There were brothels in the colonies, and women were so scarce that men would marry them anyway, no matter what their past. Most prospered, however, found good situations and some the decent husband they had hoped for. Mr. Dickens and Miss Burdett-Coutts were delighted when they received a good report or even a letter from the girl herself.

I was never entirely comfortable at Urania Cottage, and I think I would have been quite lonely if I hadn't been so busy. Mrs. Dickens had pressed me to come and visit after I returned to London, and I did call, once or twice, but Charley was away at school and none of the other children remembered me. Miss Georgina, firmly ensconced at Devonshire Terrace and as bossy as ever, was politely rude, both to me and about Urania Cottage.

"I cannot understand why Charles is so involved in the place; he is too kind-hearted, and, what with his many family responsibilities and his writing, I fear his health is suffering."

Mrs. Dickens smiled. "Did you ever know Charles to do anything he didn't want to do?"

"Be that as it may, this home is taking up far too much of his time. And quite frankly I don't think the leopard can change its spots or the lioness her nature. The whole experiment is a waste of time and money." She sighed. "Charles always wants to think the best of everybody, even prostitutes."

I spoke up. "Not all of the women are prostitutes, Miss Georgina. Some have been taken up for shoplifting or even for attempting suicide. I think he wants to see if, with kindness, with a roof over their heads, enough to eat and some instruction, they can't rise above what's happened in the past. He calls it tempting them to virtue instead of vice."

She gave me her little smile, as if to say, yes, well you *would* say that.

Neither she nor Mrs. Dickens ever came to Urania Cottage to see for themselves, but he may have asked them not to; I had told him about the fashionable ladies and our humiliating Sunday dinners.

I look long walks on my days off, sometimes ending in Kensington Gardens, reading a book if the weather were fine or tatting as I watched the children steering their toy yachts with long poles. It seemed to me that I was fated, to a great extent, to be a looker-on at life, and I tried to be content with that. There was a ragged old man who often came to the gardens — I suspect he was there every day — and he always had stale crusts or broken bits of pastry for the birds. I think this was his way of lightening his loneliness. He could set out with a definite goal — "I must go and feed my ducks; they will be expecting me" — thus giving shape to his day. Others, young and old, unemployed or unemployable, sat on the benches and simply stared straight ahead. I would never allow myself to become like that. I could always go back to Shere and find something to do there, needlework until my eyes gave out, minding children. I was paid by Mr. Dickens every quarter, and I put half my wages in the savings bank, against the time when I would return home. I also sold some of my collars and cuffs to the shop on Southampton Row, so I did not think I would ever sink to abject poverty. Nevertheless I carried a purseful of coppers with me every week for the beggars, not because I could spare the money or even because I was overly kind. It was superstitious insurance, the way Mr. Dickens touched things three times, for luck. Or, as the Bible says, "Cast thy bread upon the waters: for thou shalt find it after many days."

Elisabeth Avis came to us in our third year and was troublesome right from the start. She was neither a prostitute nor a thief but a starving needlewoman who had been arrested for stealing a footstool from her lodgings and attempting to pawn it. Her argument to the magistrate had been that she had repaired the cover and even replaced the trim around the edge, and since she had never been paid for either, she had a perfect right to pawn the thing and get her money that way. The landlady, when called upon to testify, said her lodger had had her rent reduced in the month when she made the repairs and was then in arrears for three months running. Elisabeth was sentenced to Bridewell Prison for one year. Mr. Dickens, having interviewed her and been told of her model behaviour while in prison, decided to admit her.

"She says she is a clergyman's daughter," he remarked, "and certainly her manners are a cut above the usual. But these women, whatever their crime, often say they are the daughters of clergymen. It is almost a standard reply."

What she was, it soon became clear, was a moaner and a troublemaker. It appears that she had been mistreated since childhood, when her clergyman father and his wife had drowned in a boating accident and she was sent to live with an ancient aunt.

"I could tell straightaway, for I was a sensitive and perceptive child, that this woman only took me in because she had to, and loved me far less than she loved her little lapdog. I was left almost entirely in the care of her maid, who pulled my hair when she brushed it every morning. When I complained, she said if I would only keep still, it wouldn't happen. In the park she often walked too fast in an attempt to lose me. What she would have told my great-aunt if she had succeeded, I don't know, but I was on to her tricks and ran to keep up.

"When I was ten, I was sent to a boarding school. On my very first day the headmistress called the school together, introduced me and said she hoped they would all be 'especially nice' because I had lost my father and mother at an early age. Well, I'm sure you know enough of girls to guess what happened. They were nice enough to my face, linked arms with me in the playground, offered me ribbons for my hair — I knew this was only a way of calling attention to its mousey colour — but they talked about me behind my back, made fun of my old-fashioned Sunday clothes, picked out for me by my great-aunt's maid, and my inability to name the seven greatest rivers in the world. In fact my education had been almost non-existent, and at first I had to take my lessons with the younger girls. Since I was already tall for my age, I suffered even more humiliation."

On and on she went, reciting a catalogue of the grievances and outrages that had been practised against her. This usually took place in the early evening, while Matron and I enjoyed a cup of tea in our sitting room before joining the girls for readings from Wordsworth, Crabbe, John Bunyan and the Bible. The girls liked to be read to, and it seemed to calm them down before bedtime. But now Elisabeth would think of an excuse to join us — usually a question about rules and regulations, which would lead to a hint dropped about violations of same by some girl or other, "naming no names," and that done, she would take up the narrative of her past life. She never sat down, but towered over us like a smokestack, emitting clouds of self-pity and self-importance. After several minutes of this she would say, "I must not take up any more of your valuable time with my poor story" and disappear.

Mr. Dickens confessed that she did the same to him on his weekly visits.

"And how does she get on with the other girls?" he asked.

"She doesn't. She puts on too many airs. They call her 'Betty' and 'Betsey' when she insists on 'Elisabeth.' It drives her wild."

The one redeeming feature of Elisabeth Avis was her needlework. I was quite competent, very good, in fact, thanks to Mother and the sewing mistress at the Foundling, but Elisabeth was inspired. Of course she rejected praise with false modesty, but I could tell she was pleased. She made a beautiful teacloth with roses at every corner so real you could almost smell them. We saved it for the weekly visits of Mr. Dickens and the occasional visits of Miss Burdett-Coutts. She made bookmarks for Matron and me, with suitable Biblical quotations. (Mine was from the story of the Queen of Sheba: "She came to prove him with hard questions.") I had been teaching the needlework classes, but now I asked her if she wouldn't like to do it. We would put aside a small allowance for her every week, and then, when her year was up, she would have a bit of extra money.

"Oh no!" she said, "I could not possibly set myself above the other girls" — exactly what she had been doing since the day she arrived.

It was the vicar at the new church of St. Stephen who saved the day. Because of some distant connection with Miss Burdett-Coutts, he knew about the home and asked if he could call. Somehow the subject got around to the need for kneelers and the lack of skill among his female parishioners. He did not have the funds to send out for them and yet he dearly wanted his church to look as well turned-out, as he put it, as the other churches in Shepherd's Bush.

We told him about Elisabeth, called her in, and he commissioned her on the spot. It would have to be a labour of love, he explained, with very little money attached to it, but if she were willing he would be delighted. She bowed her head and put on her most humble manner, used words like "unworthy" and "high honour" and so on, but of course she agreed to do it. Her designs would be submitted to the vicar, and, he said, he had a few ideas of his own. If she would think about hers, he would think about his, and he would come back for a consultation within the week.

Mr. Dickens thought it was an excellent idea.

Right from the beginning the undertaking went very well. Matron and I asked Elisabeth to choose other girls as helpers. At first she refused, insisting she could manage all the work by herself, but we said no, it was too much for any one person, and she would not be excused from her regular lessons and chores. She could direct the work and do the most difficult designs, she would choose the colours (the kneelers were to be done in crewel work), but others would help with backgrounds and the simpler stitches.

The project was soon underway. Matron and Mr. Dickens went off with a list of supplies to be purchased, and one large chest of drawers was turned over to the kneelers. Some of the designs were quite simple, working off the theme of Shepherd's Bush, with lambs and shepherds' crooks; others were more elaborate. The most astonishing, worked entirely by Elisabeth herself, were the four Evangelists: Matthew as the Angel, Mark with the Lion, Luke with the Ox and John with the Eagle. In brilliant reds, blues and greens, the designs throbbed with colour, unlike anything I had ever seen. The vicar called Elisabeth a true artist, and even girls who thought she was too uppity to be bothered with told her her saints were "smashin'." The only one that caused any of us discomfort was the figure of St. Stephen himself in his agony. The figures of the Jews were almost caricatures, and the saint bled copiously where the stones had broken his flesh. The vicar suggested that perhaps it inclined too much in the Roman direction, bleeding Christs and so forth. Mr. Dickens and Miss Burdett-Coutts, who had come to admire the finished work, tended to agree, but they left it up to the vicar to decide what to do.

"Amazing," Mr. Dickens said to Matron and me later, "that all that self-tormenting, all that anger, could be translated into such beauty. Miss Burdett-Coutts suggested to me that she write to the Bishop of Adelaide to see if they can make a special effort to find her suitable employment once she's out there. We think she would be wasted as a domestic."

"Could she not stay in England?"

"We considered that, but no. The whole idea behind Urania Cottage is that these girls are to be given a chance at a new life somewhere else. Even singling her out for special attention is bending the rules. However, it is up to the Bishop; he can treat her the same as the others if he so wishes."

When all the kneelers had been attached to their boards and installed in the church, the vicar invited us to a private service of thanksgiving. Mr. Dickens and Miss Burdett-Coutts attended, and Mr. Hullah, who had been hired to teach singing. Afterwards we took tea in the vicarage with the vicar and his wife and their two daughters. Elisabeth barely uttered a word, even though she was really the guest of honour. She refused cake and sat by herself on the very edge of her chair. The more she was praised, the more she seemed to shrink. When we returned home, she went immediately to her room, pleading a headache.

Matron was very worried, but one of the girls hit upon the real reason for this behaviour: "Betsey's sweet on the Vicar. She didn't know he was married." True or not, Elisabeth soon slipped back into her old, dour ways.

The episode was forgotten in the great scandal of the following month: three girls, led by Jemima Hiscock — always a difficult, argumentative girl, she would never earn her £2 for good marks — broke down the door of our beer-cellar and drank themselves silly. It was past bedtime when they crept downstairs and did this, so the rest of us awakened from sleep to a great hullabaloo of shouting, cursing and hysterical laughter. Mrs. Morton told me to dress quickly and run for the gardener, who slept in his quarters at the back of the property.

Commanding the rest of the girls to return to their rooms or lose marks for bad behaviour — for of course they came rushing out to see what was happening — Matron, the gardener and I got the miscreants to bed, not without struggles, curses and kicks. We locked them in and sent for Mr. Dickens in the morning. He dismissed them immediately, after the usual tearful scenes and vows of repentance.

Mr. Dickens always seemed terribly depressed when things like this happened, as though he were personally responsible. I suppose, because he considered himself an excellent judge of character, he did take the blow personally.

"Well," said Mavis Benson, "there's three what won't see the Southern Cross."

10

In 1851, the Great Exhibition opened at the Crystal Palace. Mr. Dickens was on some committee to do with it but resigned because he felt the common labourer would not be fairly represented. He was quite cross and somewhat cynical about the whole affair. Why not have a companion exhibition, he said: "England's Sins and Negligences: Crime, Disease and Poverty." He did attend, however, more than once, but found there was too much to look at; each time he came away with a headache. And months before the exhibition opened, he began receiving letters from people who were coming to London and would like to meet him.

"At the risk of turning into a Great Exhibition myself," he told us, "I have let the house and sent the family down to Broadstairs, where I shall join them later. Meanwhile I am hiding out at the office of *Household Words*."

In spite of his negative attitude, it was a fact that the whole world was talking about the wonders of the Crystal Palace. Matron wrote to Miss Burdett-Coutts, via Mr. Dickens (for we knew he made all the decisions), and asked if it would be possible for the inhabitants of Urania Cottage to attend when the entrance fee went down in July. The answer was yes. Matron and I and the "five best-behaved girls" would be allowed to attend. "If we are to send them out into the Great Beyond, perhaps it is as well to let them have a taste of it now. But the crowds will be fierce — you must not let them become separated from you. And do not inform them now that only the five best will be chosen or they will all put in extra effort for the wrong reasons. Just look at the marks sheets for the previous fortnight and select the girls with the highest marks."

When the time came, we did this, not without loud grumbling from the other seven, who were placated only by the possibility of an expedition later on if they behaved well now. Bribery, yes, but bribery seemed preferable to facing outright mutiny. Mr. Dickens offered to take charge personally at the cottage that day.

We took an omnibus down to the park, paid our shillings and went inside. After the quiet of Urania Cottage, the noise, at first, was almost overwhelming, and the girls appeared stunned, unable to move forward into the Great Hall. However, that passed soon enough, and we had all we could do to keep track of them as they rushed from one exhibit to the next.

I think the favourites were the stuffed elephant with the howdah on its back ("fancy ridin' around in one o' them things!") and the hydro-incubator with its hundreds of baby chicks milling about and piping. When I steered them towards the Australian, South African and Canadian exhibits, they expressed great interest in the clever kangaroo, who carried her baby in a pouch, and in snowshoes and sleighs, an elephant's foot made into an umbrella stand, a sheepskin rug. We all laughed at an American bed which, at a set time, tipped the sleeper out of bed and into a cold bath.

On the whole I thought the girls behaved themselves very well. May Corbett whispered to me (with a quick nod of her head) that the man "over there" was a pickpocket she had known in the old days. She insisted we inform a policeman, who said he would keep an eye on him. Annie Clapp said her feet were killin' her and she had a mind to take her shoes off and stick her feet in the fountain. Fortunately the laughter of her companions put an end to that idea. "I weren't really goin' to do it, I were only thinkin' how nice it would feel." We each had a saveloy and a bun and, later on, a flavoured ice, all paid for by Mr. Dickens, who said a day without treats was not a true day out.

The girls looked down their noses at the country people, wearing rosettes and led by serious-looking clergymen, and the crowds of charity children, whose entrance fees, a notice informed us, had been paid by "wealthy philanthropists who wish to remain anonymous." No doubt Mr. Dickens was one of those wealthy philanthropists. Just as we were leaving, I saw a group of boys in the uniform of the Foundling Hospital. They looked so quaint, many people were staring at them and pointing. I wondered if the girls would be allowed to come. Thank heavens *our* girls, in their varicoloured dresses, could have been a group of working-class young women from anywhere.

Back at the house our five best girls turned into our five worst girls, alternating bragging about all they had seen with sulks and mutterings about the dullness of cottage life. Worse than that, the very next night two of those girls tried to run away by pulling off the palings at one side of the garden. The gardener heard them and brought them back, and they were let off with a warning.

"What do you think," said Mr. Dickens, "of a very big dog in a barrel, at the side which leads on to the street? We would always know, then, if somebody were trying to get out — or in." The idea was never taken up — a big dog in a barrel? — and, in fact, we did not see him for a while. He was finishing a book, and his ninth child, a little girl, died very suddenly. Mrs. Dickens was away taking a cure, and he had to summon her home. My foster mother's babies, the ones who slept under the little green mounds in the Shere churchyard, never lived more than a fortnight. Dora was almost a year old; how horrible that must have been for them all. Mother told me once that you accept it — "The back is made for its burthen" — but you never get over it.

In a way I didn't blame the girls who tried to break out. They had had a taste of freedom, a taste of London, and returning to Urania Cottage must have seemed almost like a return to prison. The gardener said he was sure he had heard men's voices mixed with the girls', but they swore this wasn't so, and Mr. Dickens chose to believe them. I couldn't help wondering if they hadn't found a way to contact old friends while examining the delights of the exhibition.

I too was feeling restless, and I thought once again of trying to emigrate. I was sure Miss Burdett-Coutts would help me and might even aid me in making inquiries about Sam. Why hadn't I thought of that before? Perhaps I could chaperone the next lot who were going out. I hated the idea of being a servant again, but it might not be so bad in a new country where everyone — or almost everyone — had to start from scratch. Or perhaps I could teach, why not? I became quite excited by the idea, imagined myself in a little one-room schoolhouse in the bush, kangaroos hopping past the windows as I taught the times tables to the children of convicts and officers.

I soon became obsessed with this idea, and on my days off I walked farther and farther afield, talking to myself as I weighed the pros and cons. I had made up my mind to speak to Mr.

Dickens about it before the year was out, when one day I found myself by the bird market near Covent Garden. When Urania Cottage had first opened, Matron had a little canary in a cage, and the girls were all very fond of it until it died. Ori was an older cat now, no longer so playful. All he wanted to do was lie in the sunniest window and doze, occasionally opening one green eye to look out. Why not buy another canary for the home?

As soon as it became obvious that I was a potential customer, boys and men surrounded me, all claiming to have the most marvellous singers, the best lookers, the finest this and the finest that. ("A pair of lovebirds, Missus, now wouldn't that be a treat?" "A thrush, Miss, the children loves a thrush, there's no greater singin' bird in England than a throstle." "A singing lark?" "A goldfinch, Missus? A goldfinch is long-lived, will pair with a canary, he's fancied by the ladies.") They thrust the cages at me, all shouting at once.

And then I saw him, at the back of the crowd! I wasn't sure at first; it had been twenty-four years since I had seen him last, almost twenty-three since Sam had called out to him to run. When he looked at me and smiled, I was sure of it. I pushed my way through to him and touched his arm.

"Jonnie?" I said. He drew away quickly, shaking his head.

"Me name's Archie," he said, and turned from me.

"It's all right," I said softly, touching his arm again gently. "It's me, Harriet."

And still he looked puzzled.

"Hattie," I said, "it's Hattie."

The other sellers dropped away, not without comment — "Is she yer bird, then, Archie?" "Is she yer sweetheart?" — but he ignored them. Setting the cage down carefully, he said, "Hattie, is it really you?"

"It really is."

We fell into one another's arms.

Mr. Dickens was horrified.

"You really want to do this, Harriet? Go and live in St. Luke's in some run-down hovel in a street of rundown hovels just to be with this long-lost foster brother of yours?"

"He's family, sir, all the family I've got."

"But Lord, woman, his life has been so very different from yours! His has been a life of the streets, a rough, hand-to-mouth existence. I know, I've talked to many birdhawkers. You will eat coarse bread and drink weak tea and count yourself lucky if you see meat once a week. You are above all this; you are practically a lady."

"I'm a Foundling, sir. Jonnie was my childhood playmate, the constant companion of my early years. It broke my mother's heart when Sam was transported and Jonnie fled. Now that he's found, she'd want me to care for him in any way I can. What I am hoping is that, perhaps in a year or two, once we have become reacquainted with one another, we might be able to emigrate. I had been thinking along the lines of emigration when I met him."

"Why isn't he married, with his own woman to look after him?"

"I don't know. I haven't asked him. What I do know is that he has had a hard and lonely time, always fearing that someday a policeman's hand would fall heavily on his shoulder. And he blames himself that Sam got caught. Sam hadn't wanted to take him along that night, but Jonnie carried on until Sam relented, and he says Sam was paying too much attention to him and not enough to where he was walking."

"Sam shouldn't have been poaching."

"I know, sir, but times were hard. Our parents didn't like it, but many boys did it, men as well. With Sam it was only rabbits at first, Jonnie says, he never took the game birds until just before he was caught."

"Jonnie says. Well, I can't stop you, of course, but I think you are making a mistake. You have worked hard to get where you are. One should always move forward, never backward."

"Forward to what, sir?"

"Well . . . I don't know. Don't you want to marry one day soon and raise a family, have a home of your own?"

"I am twenty-nine years old; I suspect that future is not open to me."

"Don't be so sure — a handsome, intelligent woman like yourself. Many men would be proud to have you for a wife. I think your emigration idea was an excellent one, but on your own, unencumbered by your foster brother. Miss Burdett-Coutts and I can help you. A new country, eh? A new start?"

"Not without my brother, sir, and not right away."

"Oh very well. You have always been a stubborn miss. Go and live amongst the bird-droppings and bad language. But promise me you will leave your money in the savings bank for now and that you will let us know if you change your mind."

"Yes, sir."

He sighed. "You always seem to be leaving me, Harriet, but no doubt we shall meet again. And by the way — I thought you weren't fond of birds."

"Only ravens, sir."

And so once again I packed up my little trunk and set out on a new adventure. It was hard to leave Urania Cottage. Whatever I had originally thought about the experiment, most of the girls had lasted out their year and emigrated successfully. A few had even married. I was proud to have played a part in its success.

Ori I left behind. He was happy at the cottage and, even at his age, I did not think he would be welcome in the bird-hawkers' world.

"I usually goes alone," he said, "because this job wants utter silence, Hat. Once we sets the nets, you keep mum, understand?"

We had risen before daybreak, the nets and all our apparatus in a large basket Jonnie wore on his back. I held the callbird in a covered cage. We had walked miles before he nodded to me and said, looking across to a far field with some trees beyond, "That will do nicely." We stopped to share some bread and cheese and ale, then set off to erect the great net which would ensnare the birds. When all was ready, Jonnie told me to place the callbird carefully in the centre.

"Now," Jonnie whispered, "now we wait."

We withdrew to a safe distance away, about thirty yards, and lay flat on our bellies, with a piece of canvas under us to keep off the damp. Side by side, not speaking, hardly breathing.

My previous life, all my previous lives, seemed to have fallen away from me like the shed skins of a snake. I had always been living with my foster brother in a little two-room dwelling — it would be wrong to glorify it with the name of house — sharing it with a crippled man who made cages. I had always slept on a flock bed and awakened to a bedlam of birdsong. I had always sat on the stoop of an evening, trying to read a little while Jonnie/Archie went off for a pint with his mates. I had always drawn water at a common standpipe; I had never felt completely clean. None of this mattered because here I was with my long-lost brother, lying beside him, waiting for dawn. On a sudden impulse I reached over and touched his hand; he turned to me and whispered, "This is the life, ain't it?"

As soon as the sun rose, our callbird began his merry song, and after a while we watched the wild birds began to arrive, first in ones and twos, then more and more. When he felt that he had a sufficient quantity, Jonnie quickly drew the pull-line towards him, the wings of the net collapsed and all the birds were trapped in its folds. He showed me how to pick them off gently and transfer them to a large collapsible cage he had brought in his basket.

The callbird continued to sing, unaware of what he had done.

When I held a bird in my cupped hands, I could feel its frantic heart beating and I nearly let it go. If this work had been for anyone but Jonnie, I would have turned and run. I was sorry now that I had come out with him, and I knew I would not come again. It was not for me to judge him; this was how my brother kept himself. Yet I was sickened by the sight of those creatures of the air, tricked into captivity, who would never again roam the sky but sit in some window, caged, singing for the amusement of their jailers.

Jonnie was delighted with the pull — more than seventy-five young birds — and he whistled as we tramped back into the city. He did not notice my silence. (And the birds were silent too, had stopped their frantic beating against the cage. The callbird was once again covered up.)

"We've been lucky today, Hattie. These should fetch a good price."

Almost half the birds died in the first two days. The survivors hung in cages which covered the walls of our second room: linnets, bullfinches, all the songbirds. From these Jonnie selected the very best and trained them to sing. The rest he sold to dealers and in the markets.

"Now 'ere's where you can help, Hattie, 'ere's where you can be most useful to me. See this 'ere?" He held up a flat object with a hole at one end. "Now this 'ere is our bird organ, and it's what we teach the birds to sing with. Watch and listen for a while, you'll soon get the knack of it. I'm known around town for 'avin' the very best singin' birds, I has a reputation for it."

The bullfinches were his specialty, and once they were old enough to whistle, he placed them aside in a little darkened cupboard and fed them infrequently. Then he brought them out and played over and over the notes he wanted them to learn. When one began to sing, he was fed, and then the next commenced, and so on.

By listening attentively I found I could whistle any bird's song without the aid of the bird organ, and the birds responded well to me. Jonnie was delighted. "Why Hat, yer worth your weight in gold, you are! What you've got is a gift."

A singing bullfinch could go for as much as three guineas, but the ordinary little goldfinches were his stock in trade. They were pretty and long-lived and affordable, never costing more than a shilling.

He also carried canaries, which he bought from another fellow. "They don't mind bein' caged up, Hat, they're bred to it."

The only birds he wouldn't touch were sparrows. The

hawkers tied strings to their legs and sold them as playthings to children. "And you know what 'appens to them then, don't you? Teased and tortured until they die. There's a great trade in sparrows — quick money to be made there — but I draws the line at sparrows."

I discovered that Jonnie could barely read — fingerposts, mostly, as he tramped around bird-catching to Highgate, Richmond, Epping Forest, or signs over shops in the areas he frequented (he liked the signs with pictures best; it wasn't hard to find the Blue Boar if the boar was right there on the sign) — and it was the same for writing. I offered to teach him to read, but he said, "Why?" He could add with the best of them and find his way to and from all the places he needed to go, and that was enough.

"Besides, Hat, I'm not much of a person for sittin' still. I don't have time for it in my business. Early to bed and early to rise, that's my motto."

I never went hawking the birds but stopped at home, did the washing and sweeping, worked for hours at training our singers — I called them my choir — and talked to the crippled man who made cages for the neighbourhood.

One night I asked my brother, "Do you like this business, Jonnie?"

"It's a long day's work and a long walk 'ome when you've done the catchin', but it's the only life for me. Besides, I'm forced to like it, ain't I? I got no other trade to live by." He smiled. "And when I'm lyin' out there, I think."

"What do you think about?"

"I dunno. Nothin' perhaps. Sometimes about Father and Mother, but that makes me sad, so I try not to think that way. I thinks about God, sometimes."

"About God?"

"Yes. It seems to me that when they say God watches over everybody — if you'd spent any time in the workhouse or in a shelter, you'd know that's a constant refrain with the Bible-thumpers — well, I think it means just that. 'E watches us, but don't interfere. 'E just lets us get on with it, like, and our fate is in our own 'ands, not 'is. Then at Judgement Day, when we all 'as to line up and 'E weighs our sins, well, whether we flies or fries, it's been entirely up to us."

He was so solemn, saying all this, that I wanted to throw my arms around him and comfort him somehow, but he tended to shy away from such shows of affection. His own tenderness came out in his treatment of the birds, although, of course, he was quite cold-blooded about catching them. But once they were caught he talked to them constantly — the ones he kept for his singing school — and was saddened when any died.

Covent Garden was his usual place, but he went all over London — Smithfield, Clerkenwell-Green, the City, Shore-ditch, Spitalfields, Whitechapel, Tower Hill, Docklands. He carried the birds in wicker cages, which he sometimes fastened to a railing near one of the great parks. When he arrived home of an evening he could hardly wait to take his boots off. When I saw his poor swollen feet, I decided to invest in a big enamel basin, which I had ready with warm water as soon as I heard his step. "Ah, Hattie, you'll make me soft." But I could see that he was pleased.

The room we lived in was furnished very simply: a bed and my flock bed, a table, two chairs and a stool, a fender, a few pots and pans, some crocks. In the other room were empty cages of all sizes, sacks of various seeds and feed, the caged birds we were training to sing and the birds he was presently hawking.

We had one lamp, with a cracked chimney, and a few candles. The cripple lived in a kind of lean-to off the side of our rooms. Sometimes he shared our meals, sometimes not.

One night Jonnie said, out of the blue, "It's amazin' what a difference a woman's touch makes to a 'ouse. I had a woman once, a nice lass, but she went off with a cabbie, said she were sick and tired of birds, birds, birds. I told 'er I 'oped she liked 'orses, 'orses, 'orses, and cleanin' cages might turn out to be more pleasant than muckin' out stables, but she just tossed 'er 'ead and off she went. We wasn't together all that long and there weren't children, thank the Lord. I wouldn't 'ave let her run off like that if there 'ad been children. Some of them cab drivers is pretty rough, for all their yes sir and no sir to their fares. I knew one who beat 'is wife with the same whip he used on 'is 'orse."

"And you never wanted to marry again?"

"Well I'm still married, ain't I? If I wanted to marry again I'd 'ave to seek 'er out and go through all the legal nonsense. I couldn't afford all that, and besides, I 'ates wrangles. Things are best left alone, although I don't mind tellin' you I wasn't 'alf lonely when she first went. Still, I got over that — as Mother used to say, the back is made for its burthen — and now here you are, when I never expected to see you again in this life."

The crippled man was called "Old Albert," even though he wasn't old at all, maybe just a year or two past twenty. He was born a cripple, but his father never made him feel like a burden. He remembered his father taking him to bathe in the sea, hoping it would do some good, but nothing helped, and when he was twelve his father put him to the bird trade. However, it was very hard for him to move about, the other street-sellers mocked him, and the children teased him. His father died (he thought his mother had died at his birth) and he ended up in the workhouse.

"I was there for six months, Miss Hattie, and I vowed I would never go back, I would rather starve. And starve I did, many a day, until I met your brother, and he brought me here. He saw me fall down in the street, for want of food. His wife had left, and he put me to minding the shop and keeping the birds company while he was abroad. Then one day I picked up a broken cage and mended it and then another. He suggested I try making a few, and I discovered I had a knack for it. So he bought the necessary and set me up as a birdcage maker. I work for the whole neighbourhood now, and I never been happier. The children round here never tease me, for your brother has told them he'll do for them if they dare."

As he talked, he took wet willow out of a pan and fashioned it into a pretty basketcage for a thrush. My brother insisted upon paying him for every cage, and then, very solemnly, Old Albert would hand over a sum for materials and rent. He purchased his dinner at a public house and on Saturdays treated himself to a meat pie. He could read — I suppose his father must have taught him — and read his Bible every day. He believed most fervently in Heaven and Hell, and if he heard of an itinerant preacher anywhere nearby, he would make a slow and painful journey to listen to him and come back refreshed.

More than once Jonnie offered to take me with him again when he went bird-catching, but I couldn't do it; my hands still tingled from those frantic, beating hearts. I did not try to explain this to him but I think he understood. Nevertheless, I always awoke on a night when he was going to seek out birds. He usually started around two in the morning in order to get to his place before daylight and have time to set the net. However quietly he slipped from his bed or however carefully he gathered his traps together, I always arose, put a shawl around myself and saw him off. Perhaps I had a fear that something might happen to him and I would never see him again, I don't know. Sometimes I stood at the door and waited until he had disappeared around the corner. London was very still at that hour, in the district where we lived; it was hard to believe that in just a few hours the streets would be full of noise. In those hours before dawn I often lit a candle and went back to my bed with a book, for although, in the end I had stored most of my belongings in the box room at Urania Cottage, I had carried my precious books with me. It did not matter to me that I had read them before, many times before; just the act of reading soothed me, the sound of the words in my head. After a while I snuffed the candle and settled down again to sleep.

11

Once a year, I travelled home to visit Mother and Father's graves and spend some quiet hours in the churchyard. Now I asked Jonnie if he would go with me. I could see, from the moment the sentence was out of my mouth, that the very idea of going back in broad daylight frightened him.

"It's been years," I said. "Surely no one would ever arrest you now?"

"I can't chance it, Hat, I couldn't bear to be locked up. Just the thought of it . . ."

And so I went alone, stood in the pale winter sunshine saying my prayers for the souls of my family. Then I went into the church and sat for a while, not praying, not thinking, just glad to be there, glad, I suppose, that nothing had changed. In a little while I would visit the school, take a walk on the Downs and gather some holly for Mother's grave. Although the church smelled a bit musty — it was very old — the air was much better than the fug of London. I was almost asleep when hurrying footsteps came up behind me. It was the curate, wringing his pale hands in his usual nervous manner.

"Miss Harriet, thank heavens! I thought I had missed you."

I was dismayed that my quiet time had been interrupted,

and I suppose it showed, for he said, "I would not normally bother someone so deep in contemplation, but my wife said she saw you in the churchyard and then you disappeared."

He's going to invite me to tea, I thought, and I don't want to go to tea, I want to walk on the Downs. I wished he hadn't come looking for me; there would be no way to get out of tea and small talk without hurting his feelings — or his wife's feelings. No doubt she was already putting the kettle on, getting out a nice tea cloth and wondering if she should slice some bread and butter or if the fruitcake would be enough. What would she say if I told her I now live in a dwelling with half a hundred birds and a dirt floor?

". . . message for you." He had obviously been speaking to me and was waiting for some response.

"I'm so sorry. What did you say?"

"I have a message for you. The Misses Bray are away until the new year or I should have left it with them. I know you write to them."

"A message?" It had to be Mr. Dickens, but he knew I was in London.

"A stranger. I think he was a foreigner, although he spoke English perfectly well. From the colonies, perhaps."

My heart began to pound.

"What was the message? What did he want?"

"He wanted to find you."

"Did he leave his name? Where I could find him?" I practically grabbed the poor man by the arm.

"He left a letter, in case you came here. And another for the Misses Bray. If you just step over to the house I'll get it for you."

I nearly pushed him out of the church door, I was so eager to get my hands on that letter. Nearly tore it out of his hands. And it was as I had hoped. Sam had come home and was looking for Jonnie and me!

Perhaps Jonnie was right — that all God does is watch — for the next few weeks were among the happiest and saddest in my life thus far. I hurried back to London, refusing even a cup of tea with the curate and his wife, and went to find Sam. He had told me to write him at a lodging house not far from the India Docks. Night had fallen by the time I reached London, along with one of our dreadful fogs, a thick yellow blanket that would have made it hard to negotiate even familiar streets. I was sorry I hadn't stopped to get Jonnie first, for this was a rough district, and to the men who frequented the area — sailors mostly or longshoremen as well as thieves and those who dragged for the drowned — a woman walking alone at night, even if she were hurrying and not loitering, could want only one thing.

"Hello, darlin', lookin' for comp'ny?"

A foot without a body would suddenly appear and disappear, a hand reaching out of a filthy coat, voices, the sound of water slapping against wood. Twice I was sure I was being followed — weren't those heavy footsteps I heard behind me? — and l walked faster, terrified of the hands that would grab me, of the rag thrust into my mouth. The whole world seemed to have turned evil. Men's laughter behind the dull glow of a public house window, the sudden cackle of a woman's voice — these increased my pace until I was almost running.

With some difficulty, for I did not want to stop and ask directions, I found the address and pounded on the door. No one came for what seemed a very long time, and I was about to turn away in despair when a slatternly girl of about fifteen opened the door halfway, peered out and demanded to know what I wanted. She held up a battered tin candlestick, and the light from it made her face look old and evil.

"Do you have a lodger here? Mr. Samuel Allen? I've come to see him. I'm his sister."

"I dunno."

"Well, could you go and fetch someone who would know?"

"The mistress is busy."

I held out a sixpence.

"Please, it's important."

She took the money and shut the door in my face. I stood on the step, shivering. The fog wrapped around me, thick and greasy, and the cold made my bones ache.

I don't know how long I stood there, but I was determined to wait all night if necessary, in spite of the fog and the chill. Eventually the door opened and the girl beckoned me into a dingy hall.

"'E's in the parlour."

"Did you tell him his sister was here?"

"I didn't tell 'im nuffink. I just got 'im for you."

"He doesn't know I'm here?"

She shrugged. "You can go tell 'im yerself."

My hand trembled on the knob. What would I find when I opened the door? I could hear men's voices, so more than one man awaited me. The letter had been brief but well-written, yet this seemed such a low place. Perhaps he had gone to a scrivener and could not write himself.

"Well," said the girl, "are yer going in or not?"

I knocked and went in.

Four men played cards by lamplight. The three who could see the door looked up in surprise.

"Hello, hello," said one, "who's this?"

They were big men, rough-looking men, stevedores or bargemen.

"Whatever 'tis you're offerin'," said another, "I'm buyin'," and he laughed heartily at this witticism.

"I am looking for my brother," I said, my voice trembling. "I believe he is stopping here."

The man with his back to me whirled around and stood up, knocking over his chair.

"Hattie?" he said. "Hattie?"

I would not have recognized him, this tall, muscled giant, had he not spoken my name. Then he moved towards me, and I could see that he walked with a limp.

"Sam, is it you?"

The giant began to sob, great tears rolling down his cheeks, his hands outstretched, palms upward. I, who had never fainted in my life, felt the room spin and fell to the floor.

When I regained consciousness, I was lying on an old sofa, with Sam beside me and a cool cloth on my forehead. The other men were gone. I struggled to sit up, but Sam gently pressed me down.

"Lie still for a while, Hattie, you've had a shock. We'll talk in a minute."

Still trembling and disoriented I was content to do his bidding.

"My dear, you should not have come here alone. This is not the neighbourhood for a woman like you."

"I was in Shere," I said, "visiting our parents' grave when the curate gave me your letter. I had to come. I knew I could not rest until I had seen you."

"I shall go back with you as soon as it is light."

"No, no. I do not live in the country. Did the curate not explain that to you?"

"He said very little. I think he was suspicious of me."

"Did you see their graves, Sam? Mother, Father, Grandfather?"

He bowed his head and nodded.

"I did."

I took a breath.

"Now, Sam, take my hand and hold it tight." When he had done this, I began my story. "Sam, I am living with Jonnie. He is here in London as well."

"Oh God oh God. My brother and sister found on the same day! I did not dare to inquire in the village, and Mother told me, before I was transported, that she feared he was gone forever. That has lain like a stone on my heart for all these years."

"I only discovered him quite recently, and that by accident."

I told him how I had stopped in Neal's Yard, with the idea of buying a canary, and how I had seen Jonnie in the crowd of hawkers. How he had nearly run away when I called him by his old name, for he did not recognize me.

"No more did I. You are a woman now, Hattie, and much changed. It is only your hair that is the same, and when you came in that was covered by your shawl." He twisted one of my curls around his big, work-scarred fingers.

"Oh Hattie," he said, "I have been so lonely for all of you. I thought I would never see you again."

For a while we remained silent, hands clasped.

"I want you to take me to Jonnie," he said, "but first you must eat something. I think your faint was partly from hunger. I shall leave you for a minute while I send that girl for something hot. After our breakfast, and as soon as it is light, we will be away from this place."

"There is money in the side of my shoe, if I can just unlace it."

"In the side of your shoe!"

"I feared I might be robbed."

"And so you might have been — or worse. But don't worry about money, Hattie. In spite of the surroundings in which you find me, I am well set up for money, truly I am. Australia, in the end, was kind to me. I came to stay in this low place because I had a letter to deliver to the woman who runs it, a letter from her son. Then I decided to stay a few days in case I heard from you."

"And after that?"

He limped to the door and went in search of the girl.

I lay back on the sofa — he had taken away my damp shawl and covered me with a heavy coat — and I must have fallen asleep for a while, worn out by emotion and the fatigue of my rushed journey. The next thing I knew he was back, had drawn up by my side a small table with a tray of food set upon it and a steaming jug of something that smelled of lemons and spice.

"Now you must eat — we'll both eat — and then in a few hours we'll be off. I think we have a great deal to tell one another, stories of a whole lifetime, nearly, but for the present let us just break bread together, Hattie, and try not to tell everything all at once. I'm still finding it hard to believe I'm not asleep and you nothing more than a cruel trick of my imagination."

I leaned over and pinched him. "Was that an imaginary pinch?" I said.

We bowed our heads and gave thanks to the Creator for bringing us together after all those years, and then we ate, and then I slept a little more with my brother's hand in mine.

Shortly after dawn he awakened me and settled his bill ("Yer sister!" said the girl, and gave a nasty laugh), and we set off.

"Are you feeling strong enough to walk a while, Hattie? We won't find transportation around here, not at this time of day."

I laughed. "I am a champion walker, Sam. Walking is something I'm very fond of."

The neighbourhood was perhaps less fearsome now that day had come and the fog had dissipated somewhat, but it was terribly run down, and the gutters overflowed with filth. Several times we saw rough men sleeping off the effects of the night's debauch in doorways, and once or twice a shawled figure wandering home with uneven steps from God knows where. When we reached Tower Hill we took a cab.

"Sam," I said, as we rattled along, "Jonnie bears no animosity towards you, I want you to understand that. On the contrary, he feels that if he hadn't insisted upon going along that night, you would have paid more attention to where you were walking. You would have seen the trap before you stepped in it."

"Not true, not true. And I never should have been there at all. You see, Hattie, we weren't really like the men who poached from hunger. Times were hard, but Father was never out of work and Grandfather brought in money with his carving. No, I did it chiefly for the excitement, I did it just to do it and not get caught. It didn't matter how many times Father punished me for it or Grandfather warned or Mother wept, I wanted excitement, the thrill of being on forbidden ground, of outwitting the gamekeepers. I never thought of prison, even though I knew what I was doing could lead me there, for I was far too clever to get caught. I paid dearly for my arrogance — we all did." He brushed his hand across his eyes.

"Tell the man to turn here," I said, "and then take the small street to the right."

Jonnie was just fitting the day's birds into a big cage before he left for the market. He turned in surprise as I appeared in the doorway with a stranger.

"Hattie, I'm glad yer back. There's a lady in St. John's Wood what wants a piping bullfinch. Do you think any of ours is ready?"

"Jonnie —"

"She'll pay good money, she says, for a first-rate singer. At least three guineas, mebbe more once she 'ears 'im. Choose our very best, all right, and I'll take 'im round this evening."

"Jonnie," I said, "hold on a minute. Here's someone come to see you."

Once again the momentary panic in his eyes — would there ever come a time when he would feel easy meeting strangers? (And yet he could wander all over London hawking his birds.)

The reunion between the brothers was pitiful, each taking upon himself the burden of guilt for what had happened. And when Sam removed his boots and showed us his right foot, made of wood, Jonnie broke down and sobbed like a little child.

"You must stop that, you hear," Sam said. "This is not the work of the trap but of the careless prison doctor who first fixed me up. The foot went bad on the voyage out, and there was nothing for it but to take it off. I thought surely I would die that night, and for several days after, but the Lord didn't see it that way and I hung on. By the time we arrived in Australia, I was as right as rain."

"Except that you had no foot."

"Aye, except that I had no foot. This did limit my usefulness somewhat, but I was a strong lad, foot or no foot, and so they put me to driving wagonloads of fellow convicts up and down the country, wherever they were needed, always with an officer or two, you understand, sometimes more if they figured somebody might try to escape. There is so much land out there it would be easy, if you could get away, to lose yourself, start again — if you didn't die of the rot or a snake bite or a run-in with a kangaroo. One kick to the head and you're a goner.

"The ship's carpenter had fashioned me a peg, to balance me, you know, but I found that very unsatisfactory. At night, when I couldn't sleep, I kept chewing away at the problem. Finally I thought I'd try my hand at carving an artificial foot attached to a series of straps so I could easily put it on and take it off. I begged a block of wood and began to whittle it into the shape of my missing foot." He laughed. "Of course, I was using my left foot as a model, and so the first attempt *looked* fine, but it was suitable for a man who'd lost his left foot. I had to begin all over again, and the second time I did it correct. I got quite carried away and even gave it wooden toenails and a few wooden veins. I attached a leather pad to it, just as the ship's carpenter had done for my peg, and there I was. Took a while to get used to it, after the peg, but soon I forgot about it. It wasn't much use for shovelling, but I even managed that eventually. Sometimes, when we were all sitting around a campfire at night, I'd dampen my right boot a bit, then stick it up close to the fire until it was smouldering, like, just a bit. Then I'd jump up and yell that my foot was on fire, quickly detach the braces and throw the boot, with foot attached, into the bush. The prisoners would just sit there with their jaws hanging down saying 'Jaysus Christ, Jaysus Christ,' the rest of us doubled over laughing."

I think, for Jonnie's sake, he tried to make light of his early years in Australia, but you had only to look at his face to see another story written there. And when he pulled his shirt over his head — Jonnie insisted he stay with us that night — we could see the ugly scars that criss-crossed his back.

The next day Jonnie went out hawking as usual, and then Sam left, promising to be back in the late afternoon. He had spent a while talking to Old Albert, who very much admired the artificial foot, while my brother, in turn, exclaimed over the delicacy of the bird cages. When Sam returned, he said he had removed to a lodging house nearby and had ordered a celebration dinner to be brought round at seven. From the pockets of his greatcoat he brought out knives and plates, a corkscrew, lemons and various twists of spices.

"Tonight is a joyous occasion, an occasion I never thought I'd live to see. All three of us together, all thriving." I had seen him glance more than once at our humble accommodation and frown. He had told me that morning that he had come home with plenty of money — "honest money, Hattie, honestly earned" — but I believed he would not force any changes on us until he knew us better.

12

Just a few days before Christmas, Jonnie arrived home with all his singers sold, even our shy skylark, who had so far proved unwilling to sing in public. "She gave a lovely performance, she did, and was snapped up in no time." He went out quickly to buy ale for the feast and I went around to the side to entice Old Albert to join us. His answer was, as always, "Just this once."

Oysters can be eaten perfectly well without oyster forks, and sugar lumps can be dropped into hot punch without the aid of sugar tongs. It does not matter what you eat, or what you eat it with, if you are with the ones you love. Love itself is the sauce that transforms even the simplest meal into a banquet. And this was not a simple meal: it took three boys to deliver it; the smallest looked as though his tray was far too heavy for him and he might faint on the spot. (Sam revived him with sixpences.) We began with oysters, worked our way through chops, cold beef with horseradish, jacket potatoes, oranges and nuts. Sam had forgotten to buy a nutcracker and caused great hilarity by cracking the nuts with his wooden foot. Even Old Albert laughed, such an unusual sound — a bit like a donkey braying or the squawk of ancient, rusting machinery — I thought for a moment he was choking.

"Tomorrow," Sam said, as he embraced us both and made his farewells, "tomorrow we shall talk about the future."

After he left and Old Albert had gone off to his kennel, Jonnie took my hand.

"Will you sit up with me a bit, Hattie?"

"Of course. Is something wrong?"

"No, no. 'Ow could anything be wrong on such a night? It's just . . . well . . . I would never like to leave London, it's me 'ome. Oh, I likes gettin' up in the dark and settin' out for a good tramp in the country to catch my birds, but I could never live there all the time. I likes bein' in the streets."

"I know you do, love."

"I think Sam's future don't include London."

"Why do you say that?"

"Things 'e let drop. It worries me."

"But you have a say in your own future, Jonnie. Sam may be your brother, but you are your own man. He would never force you to do anything that wasn't right for you."

"Ah, but that's just it! 'E wouldn't 'ave to force me. Do you think I want to lose 'im again — or lose you?"

"What's this talk about losing me? I told you I would never leave you."

"Times change."

"*I* don't change. And I don't break promises."

Which is why, when Sam arrived the next evening and laid out his plans for buying a bit of land in the country, in or near Shere, perhaps in Gomshall or Peaslake, of building a cottage with a room for each of us, where we could all be together in peace and contentment for the rest of our lives, I fought down my inclination to cry, "Yes, oh yes!" and told Sam that I was a London girl now and wanted to remain here, with Jonnie.

Turning to his brother, he asked, "And you wish to remain?"

"I does. One man's best suited to one place, one to another. This is what suits me."

Sam looked so disappointed, I felt pulled in two. I wanted to be with both of them, but I knew that if I told the truth about my yearning for the country, Jonnie would sell up his business and come with us like a shot. I owed it to Jonnie to keep quiet.

"Sam," I said, "now that you have found us, we shall never be far apart, whatever happens. If you have come back with the hopes of buying a small farm, I think you should do it. Surrey is not far away. We can visit back and forth all the time."

"It won't be the same."

"No, not the same, but Jonnie has built up a good business here — his singers are considered the best in London. I like helping with the singing lessons and looking after the little house. I'm used to it now."

"Very well. I'll not try to persuade you otherwise. It had always been my dream to come back and run a small farm, whether I found either of you or not, so I shall go ahead with my plan. But you must both swear that you will visit me every chance you get. Now that the line from Guildford goes through Gomshall, it is not so difficult to come out from London as in the old days. I will always be happy to pay your fares."

It being Christmastime we made merry every evening, and the whole neighbourhood was in and out to sample the punch, wish us a Happy Christmas and hear stories of Australia. Sam gave Jonnie an enormous ostrich egg, carved with the figures of the Queen and Prince Albert, looking nothing like the royal couple but wearing crowns and decorations. For me he had a pair of eardrops made of opals, unlike any opals I had ever seen before: every colour of the rainbow shone within them. He said they were from the far north of Australia, where he had never been, but he'd bought the stones off another man and had had them made up in Adelaide.

My present to both of them, to all of us, was a trip to the pantomime at Covent Garden, and Jonnie's gifts were a small cameo brooch for me and, of all things, a terrier pup for Sam. We would keep it, Jonnie said, until Sam was settled someplace. Sam named him Digger and we all fell in love with him immediately.

Sam had arranged to stay at the White Horse Inn, in Shere, while he looked around, and by the end of December he was gone.

"Are you sure, Hattie," Jonnie said to me — how quiet it seemed with Sam gone — "are you sure you don't want to go with him?"

Digger squirmed in my lap and yelped; I must have squeezed him too tightly.

"I'm sure. My place is here."

The New Year's bells rang out extra joyously that year, all over the great city. I went to church and gave thanks for our reunion and prayed that the years to come would find us never far from one another. How I wished our mother and father could know that Sam had at long last come home. The rector would no doubt assure me, "They know, my dear, they know," and I tried very hard to believe this, and believe that Grand-father was smiling up in Heaven too, but my sceptical side said that souls did not have smiles, that souls were like the winds — we could see their effects, the bent branches, the dancing flowers, the ruffled waters, but we could never see their shape.

When I came out of church, I went down to the river and walked. The fog that had covered the city in the week before

Christmas had left us for a while, and the winter sun, although shedding little warmth, cast a harsh, metallic light on the great river. There was not much river traffic on this holiday, but a few oarsmen rowed their boats under the bridges and out towards the sea. I had thought so much about emigrating with Jonnie to a new land — not Australia, I had decided, even before Sam returned, but western North America perhaps. Miss Burdett-Coutts had connections everywhere. I had imagined us sailing away from the past into a bright future, where we would build a little cabin by a stream, plant vegetables and flowers, fish for our dinners. I could see now, with Sam home, that that was out of the question. Sam was finished with travelling, he said, and Jonnie had made a life for himself in the city. I stood in the middle of Waterloo Bridge and opened my hand, consigning my dream to the water, letting the current take it. It was a small enough sacrifice to make to stay close to my family. I walked back to our mean street with no regrets. I was, I realized, a bit like one of those twig boats we had launched in the Tilling-bourne as children. I would submit myself to the stream of my life and let the current take me where it might. So long as my brothers were near me, each of us drawing strength from the other, then I would be content.

The fog that rolled in a few weeks later was not the usual acrid yellow blanket that we cursed but had learned to accept as part of London life. That we could tolerate. This was the fog of pestilence, of the dreaded cholera, and as usual it attacked the poorest and most overcrowded sections of the city. Sam urged us to come away until the danger was over, but Jonnie just laughed and said he had survived '31 and '48 and he had no intention of leaving.

"But perhaps you should go, Hattie, just for a while?"

Aside from the scarlatina, when I was a child, I had never been ill a day in my life. I decided to stay. The disease had so far left our neighbourhood alone, although people were dying by the hundreds in Seven Dials and Cheapside. Jonnie was still out catching birds every other Sunday and hawking them the rest of the week, but he promised not to go near any section of the city which harboured the disease. I stayed close to home (I had given up tatting temporarily because I felt my hands were never quite clean), tutored my singing school and attempted to train Digger, whose paws seemed to be growing much faster than the rest of him.

So how did I fall victim to this terrible thing? We never knew. It started with a piercing headache and chills in the middle of the night, then terrible cramps and violent purging. When Jonnie came home, he found me on the floor, moaning, with Digger anxiously whining beside me and licking my feet. I was too weak by then even to raise myself to my bed. I thought it must have been something I'd eaten, but Jonnie sent for the doctor immediately. He gave me paregoric and said I must drink plenty of fluids, but I could keep nothing down. I begged Jonnie to go away at once and save himself. "I'm not afraid," I whispered to him, "I'm not afraid."

By evening I had slipped into unconsciousness, and Jonnie sent Old Albert to the post office with a message for Sam to come quickly; I was dying.

Twenty-three dead on our street alone. The little boy next door, his mother and father, his grandmother. Only his sister survived. The publican and his wife. But I knew none of this then. People fleeing the city carried the illness into the suburbs. Neighbourhoods such as ours were put under quarantine in the hopes that would stop the spread of the disease. The well-to-do, who remained shut up in their houses, were, for the most part, spared.

Death moved through the nearly empty streets.

In my delirium I heard a barrel organ and could not resist my desperate urge to follow it. It took both Jonnie and Old Albert to hold me down. Sometimes I thought I was back at the Foundling and dreamed of sitting at Sunday dinner once again with the fashionable ladies mocking me.

I saw Grip; I saw a dozen ravens, all trying to bite off my eardrops and carry them away for hiding. "Tattycoram," they screamed, "Tattycoram." Some of them had human faces, with long noses and narrow chins.

I wept and confessed to sins I had not committed; I cried aloud for my mother.

Sam came and I did not know him. The doctor came again, with a white handkerchief over his nose, they said, in case he breathed in the pestilence. He gave me some pills of opium to calm me, shook his head and went away.

The opium pills seemed to make my visions even more hideous — I screamed and tore my hair — so they were abandoned. My brothers took turns sponging me and changing my linen. They burned sweet herbs to purify the air. One or another was always at my side, squeezing a few drops of brandy and water between my cracked lips.

Each day they expected to be my last — for cholera kills quickly — but there was something in me, even as I shouted and begged them to let me go, that refused to give up. On the third night the crisis passed and I fell into a deep sleep. From then on it was almost miraculous how quickly I recovered. I was soon sitting up and able to take a bit of broth, some bread and custard the day after.

But just as we were celebrating my wonderful recovery, Jonnie went down with the cholera and died the next day. We sat there beside his lifeless body, too stunned to accept what had happened.

"Why?" I kept repeating. "Why?" It should have been me.

They came and took his body away, for we were not allowed to bury him in the proper manner, the authorities by that time being so afraid of contamination. After they left, Sam said, "When the quarantine is lifted, Hattie, you must leave this place. Jonnie himself would not want you to stay here now that he is gone."

"What about the birds? I have to look after the birds."

"I think we should give the birds to Old Albert, don't you?"

"How will he sell them when he can barely walk? How will he catch more, once he has sold these?"

"I have an idea about that, which I will discuss with him. And I can give him the money to hire a boy to catch more birds. Jonnie's reputation is so high, I don't see why Old Albert couldn't sell the birds from home. We could even get a board-man to walk up and down, at first, to advertise for him. Old Albert could sell only to the dealers."

The crippled man, devastated by Jonnie's death, hardly came out of his hut. Sam went to talk to him and returned an hour later.

"Will he agree to it?"

"Most of it, but there is one part he wants altered."

"What is that?"

"He wants us to set free all Jonnie's birds."

"Set them free?"

"Yes. He has some idea that Jonnie won't rest until this is done."

I could not help smiling through my tears.

"Jonnie would probably say, 'I've worked bleedin' 'ard to catch and train them birds, don't you dare set them free.'"

"Well, Old Albert is of a different opinion, and I think we have to go along with it."

And so, a week later, a chaise rolled out towards Highgate with three people inside and a hundred birds in cages strapped to the top. On Highgate Hill we got out, and Sam carried the cages into a field close by the cemetery. He undid the fastenings and opened the doors.

The birds just sat there.

"Perhaps it won't work," I said. "Perhaps they've been cooped up too long."

"Aye, I've seen men like that in my time, afraid to leave the prison they are used to. You may be right."

But no, a little goldfinch hopped out onto the grass, tested its wings and flew to the top of a high bush. Then another. Then another. Thrushes and bullfinches, emitting frantic little cries, jostling each other now in their rush for freedom. It was an amazing sight. Then, some already singing, they flew away.

"Are you satisfied now, Old Albert?" Sam asked the crippled man. He nodded, too overcome to speak.

"I think we need a restorative," Sam said, "when we get back home." The cages, empty now, were once again strapped to the top of the chaise, the driver shaking his head and muttering, "Lunatics."

We drank a toast to Jonnie and then, that very afternoon, leaving Old Albert in charge of the business and with a local boy already hired to help him, we took up Digger and my few possessions (Sam had arranged for my trunk at Urania Cottage to be forwarded) and left the city for home, I in my black dress and Sam with a black band around his sleeve.

"Ah, Hattie," Sam said, "thank God we have each other."

13

And now, although my life slows down, my narrative speeds up. Sam had leased a small farm on the outskirts of Shere, near Coombe Bottom, and there we settled down to look after one another, as well as a few sheep and chickens. I added my money from the savings bank to my brother's hoard, and we were quite comfortable. Sam had inherited his grandfather's talent for carving, and although this was not his original intention, he made his living not from the sheep but from this gift that had been handed down to him. It was wonderful to see those big hands pick up a knife or a chisel and begin to fashion something, a newel post, a table leg, a screen. Most of his commissions came from the big houses round about the parish, but he also made coffins, both simple and grand. If a child died, there was always a little lamb carved into the top, and for the adults, if requested, he would create a motif that celebrated what they had been in life. When the old sexton died, Sam carved a garland of shovels. He never charged the labouring families extra for this work, although he was very businesslike with the rich folks.

We walked to church together every Sunday and then spent a quiet time in the churchyard, where there was now a little plaque honouring our brother: his name and his dates and a skylark soaring up to Heaven. There were some, newcomers as well as old families, who avoided us because Sam was a returned convict, but most welcomed us and made room for us at every festival and wake.

Digger proved hopeless as a sheep dog and so we bought a collie from a man in Guildford. Fortunately he and Digger became great friends, although there seemed to be an unspoken rule between them that when Angus was rounding up the sheep, Digger was to keep his mouth shut and follow directions.

I do not know the exact moment when I realized I felt more than a sister's love for Sam. Perhaps it had been there from the time I awoke from my swoon in that awful lodging house and found Sam holding my hand and looking down at me with such concern and tenderness. I only know that once I discovered this in myself, I was determined he should never know. He had told me of his rough life in Australia and confessed that he "had sinned as much as any man there," though he was sorry for it now.

"It's a strange thing what loneliness will do to a man, Hattie. A kind word, even from a harlot's lips, is sometimes all that keeps him going. I hope God forgives me now, and that you can find it in your heart to forgive me. I don't want you to think I'm better than I am."

"Were there many of these women out there?"

"More than enough, more than enough. When a man had done his time and was released, he had choices. If the hard work didn't kill him, it made him strong. There was plenty of land, you know. My God, was there land! Work as a labourer, a jackaroo, anything, until you had put by some ready money, and then strike out on your own. Farmers needed wives, of

course, and the strongest girls were snatched up. Claim a few
acres, buy a few sheep — lovely sheep, those merinos — and if
you had any brains at all you were on your way. And the officers'
wives needed servants, whom they tended to treat badly, by the
way. Then there were shops, but most of those were run by men.
However, there were bars in the settlements, more bars in the
towns — more bars than churches — and so there were bar-
maids, but again, these were the toughest girls, the girls who
could give as good as they got. As for the others, broken in health
or spirit, how were they to live?"

"Were there beggars, Sam?"

"Of course. What does the Bible say about the poor? That is
a land that has no time for the weak and helpless. Not many
society ladies wanting to help out there. No society ladies at all,
really, although the officers' wives and the clergymen's wives
tried to put on airs, dragging their pretty dresses through the
dirt, working at keeping their skin pale and out of the sun. The
sun in Australia is fierce."

"You never thought of staying, when your time was up?"

"I thought about it. Australia is a land of opportunity, and
except to a few, it makes no difference how you ended up there.
I did stay a while, carved out a little farm for myself — I had
become interested in sheep — but at night, once the sun had
gone down, too tired to sleep, all I could think about was home.
I wanted to find my brother, if he was still alive, and my parents,
Grandfather, you. I missed the gentle climate, the old familiar
birds, the Hurtwood, the stream.

"I could have made a go of it. I *was* making a go of it, even
if my nearest neighbour was fifty miles away on a bush road.
There are fortunes to be made out there, and it's exciting to be
in on the beginning of things. If only I could have wiped out

those memories, those yearnings. Jonnie would have loved it there, the parrots and the cockatoos, all the different birds."

"I thought of going there once," I said.

"You?"

"Yes. I knew Mr. Dickens and Miss Burdett-Coutts would help me. And once I found Jonnie, I thought about it a lot, although I had not yet mentioned it to him. I thought about North America as well, but I always hesitated. Not out of fear. I suppose it was out of the thought that you might return some day and find everyone gone. But if I hadn't run into Jonnie . . ."

He pressed my hand. "I'm glad you hesitated."

"And I am."

He smoked his pipe and whittled away at the handle of a rattle he was making for a farmer's baby. We read to one another from my small library, which Mr. Dickens had augmented every year until this last one. I had written to tell him that Jonnie was dead and Sam returned and that I was leaving London, but I had no reply. He might have been abroad again, or perhaps he now felt that his obligations to me were over. At the end of a chapter, I closed the book, took my candle, kissed Sam's forehead and went up to bed. It was a pattern established early on. He would stay downstairs for a while after I had retired for the night. Digger and Angus stayed with him, asleep at his feet. I slept so well, now, knowing he was there below.

Just after harvest time, in our third year back in the parish, there was a wedding between one of the servants at the manor house and the apprentice at the smithy. Both of these young people were very popular; the girl's mistress positively doted on her, although this had not spoiled her in any way. The old tithe barn was offered for the wedding breakfast, to which the entire neighbourhood was invited, and later on there was to be a dance.

The weather was perfect, one of those soft, smoky September days, and as the harvest had been a good one, everybody was in a celebratory mood. The bride and groom were beautiful as they walked to the church, followed by the admiring villagers, a young king and queen of the harvest, the very personification of ripeness and good health. The groom blushed more than the bride as they walked along. (I had been asked to embroider the sleeves of her simple gown, so I had worked harebells and marguerites.) Bells rang out, small boys turned cartwheels, and great cheers went up for the Lord and Lady of the Manor and their family.

After the simple service, the breakfast: cold hams and haunches of beef, plenty of ale for all, little wrapped pieces of the wedding cake for the unmarried girls to dream on.

And that night, with two fiddles playing the old tunes, the reels and jigs began. It was wonderful to see the big burly farm boys stomping their feet in perfect time to the music, stepping forward with the girls at just the right moment, joining hands and dancing up and down the line. Candles in sconces cast a buttery light, and shadow dancers copied the patterns on the walls.

Matrons danced with their husbands dressed in their very best (jackets soon to come off). In the corners little girls danced with one another, babies slept in baskets, and boys ran round and round trying to cause trouble, but no one paid them any attention.

I had been to weddings in the village before but always alone, as the teacher, sitting with the old ladies, who were already purling away in anticipation of another baby in nine months. I was never asked to dance and felt awkward and shy. This time I was sitting with my brother, my arm linked in his.

After a while the fiddlers rested, wiped their brows with their neckerchiefs, drank some ale, and then the music started up again. Sam turned to me and said, "Well, Hattie, what about it? That near set lacks a couple."

"But your foot?"

He grabbed my hand and pulled me up. "Come on."

There was nothing graceful about Sam's dancing, but he knew the figures better than I and we made it through, much to the delight of the rest of the set, who applauded us warmly.

"Great fun, but that's enough for now," Sam said, and beckoned to another couple to replace us.

Now others came up and asked me to dance. I had no idea what I was doing, but with a good partner who gave me a firm push in the right direction when necessary or a friendly wink if I stumbled a bit, I found I was thoroughly enjoying myself.

At midnight the trestle tables were set up again for supper, and shortly afterwards we left, although no doubt the dancing would go on until dawn. A harvest moon hung in the sky like a gigantic orange. There was no wind. The horned owl hooted, and nearby we heard the thin wail of Mrs. Coster's seventh son.

Sam laughed. "There'll be more of *that* around next lambing season, I shouldn't wonder."

There was a bench in front of our cottage, just as in our childhood.

"I have a great desire to smoke a pipe out here before turning in. Do you fancy keeping me company for a while?" He fetched his pipe and let the dogs out; they had been whining behind the door ever since they heard our voices.

Sam filled his pipe, lit it, took a few deep puffs and let out a sigh of contentment.

"You know, Hattie, sometimes I think it helps to have known

trouble, for then, when you experience contentment, you recognize it for what it is."

"Are you content, Sam?"

"Oh, aye. Can't you tell?" Then he paused. "Except, perhaps, for one thing."

"What is that?"

"Seeing all those merry couples tonight made me think that perhaps I should look for a wife."

It was as though the distant moon had turned to ice and a chill wind had sprung up around me. My best silk shawl seemed woefully inadequate to keep out the cold that seeped in. Somehow I managed to keep my voice steady.

"A wife?"

"Yes, a wife. What do you think of the idea? Perhaps you could help me in my search. Do you think there might be a woman in this county who would take an aging cripple as her husband?"

"You, a cripple! Who was up there dancing tonight? That was no cripple."

"One set and I was finished. And at any rate, I was only showing off. Now *you* — you were doing splendidly."

"Was I? I had never danced before in my life, except once when Mr. Dickens gave all the servants a whirl on Twelfth Night."

"Never before?"

"Never."

"Well, you are a natural and you must do more of it." He took another few draws at his pipe. "I'll tell you what, Hattie, here's an idea. Why don't we help each other? I'll seek out a dancing husband for you and you can inquire for a nice obedient wife for me. What do you think?"

I was grateful for the darkness so that he could not see my face, and yet a sob escaped me, I couldn't help it. The tears rolled down my cheeks. He turned and touched my face.

"What's this? Don't you like the idea of the dancing husband?" Another sob was all the answer I could give.

And then he said, "Oh Hattie, Hattie, it is wrong of me to tease. I want no other wife but you, my dear, but I have been afraid to ask. Tonight, when I saw you dancing and enjoying it so, I felt a new sensation — I think its name is jealousy. And not just jealousy, but despair. I vowed I would say nothing, but I could not resist testing you a bit. I didn't mean to make you cry. Could you really love a battle-scarred, weatherbeaten, one-footed man like me?"

"One heart," I said, "is all I need."

There was silence for a while after that, and then he said, "May I go and fetch you a warmer covering? I think it would be nice if we sat here a while longer and enjoyed this still moment together."

We gave ourselves a holiday the next day and took a walk on the Downs. Away in an orchard women and children on ladders were picking the last apples, and, even farther away, we heard the horn and the barking hounds, long before we saw the distant pink-coated hunters galloping madly over the landscape.

"'This is the way the gentlemen ride,'" Sam said, remembering the old game on Grandfather's knee, "only every farmer wants to be a gentleman now, and his wife must be a lady. They care nothing for their workers. Times have changed and are changing still. And now the railway cuts through the valley, the city comes to the country. We are fortunate to have skills that will be in demand for a long time to come."

"And land," I said. "No one can turn us away."

"Not for ninety-nine years, at any rate."

The banns were read and we were married quietly a few weeks later, with the Misses Bray, very old now but as generous as ever, standing up for us, along with Old Albert, whom we had brought out specially from London.

I was thirty-six years old and Sam was forty-five.

And now we went up the stairs at night together.

To our delight, the following year a little girl was born to us. As I lay in the upstairs room, panting, clutching the bedposts, I remembered the long ago day in the kitchen at Doughty Street and asking, "Is she going to die?"

Yet out of such pain, such joy. We named her Anne, after Mother, but for some reason she was called Rosie, almost from the first. She had my springy curls but Sam's colouring, hair the colour of new pennies and, in time, lots of freckles. Digger became her special protector as though to show Angus he too could round up little lambs when called upon to do so. He placed himself between her and the fender and always accompanied her on her toddling explorations of the outside world.

After Rosie there was a little boy who lived long enough to open his eyes, look blankly at his mother and father and then close them again. We named him John. He was a tiny baby and could easily have fitted in one of Sam's big shoes. His father made him a lovely coffin out of oak, and we buried him next to the rest of the family. Mother told me how people said to her, after each dead baby, "Well, it isn't as though you really knew him," and how she wanted to scream at them that if you carry a child beneath your heart for nine months, you do know it, that it has its own particular movements, its own uniqueness, right from the start. How each time she buried this child she already knew, she buried a piece of her heart.

There were no more babies after that, but we were more than content with Rosie. Down came the little chair I had sat in all those years ago; down came poor old Baby (I made her a new dress from a checked handkerchief); out came the wooden hen with her revolving egg.

"I had forgotten about that hen," Sam said, and he began making copies to sell at the annual Guildford Fair, where they were a great success. We all loved the fair, but coming home I always said, "Well, that's enough bustle for this year."

And so the years went on, the seasons came and went, and suddenly Rosie was nearly ten years old, one of the best scholars at the village school and, when at home, a great help to me, teasing and carding the wool from Sam's sheep, learning to use a spindle. And of course I taught her the pleasures of tatting and embroidery. She was a chatterbox and asked the drollest questions: "Mam, what do the cows think about when they stand there staring?"; "Mam, why does Digger only bark? Why can't he talk, like me?"

Sam said one night, after Rosie had gone up, "Ah, Hattie, isn't it grand to think that child will never have a number hung round her neck, like you, or printed across her back, like me?"

"Are we going to tell her, Sam — our history?"

"Oh yes, all of it. Nothing must be hidden. We should tell her soon, before the old gossips do."

And yet I kept putting it off; could not the past simply remain the past? I think the truth was that I did not know how to tell her about my first mother giving me up. Rosie would ask so many questions, might demand that we set off "at once" (one of her favourite phrases) to find her, whereas I had long ago given up any desire to do so. My real mother was the mother who had loved me and cared for me in Shere. As for Sam, boys and men still poached, although they were no longer transported. That Rosie would more readily understand.

14

One May day, when Sam was away to Albury, taking measurements for a grand banister to go in a new house under construction there and Rosie was at school, two strangers appeared at my open door: a tall thin woman in black shawl and bonnet and a little man, not much taller than a dwarf, also dressed in black, very rusty black. Digger and Angus had both gone off on some adventure or other, so I had no barked warning at the visitors' approach. I had been up to the shop for some lump sugar (Sam liked his tea heavily sugared) and had just put the kettle on when these two odd creatures appeared.

"Hello," I said, "are you looking for me?" The woman gave me a bold stare, then looked me up and down in an offensive way.

"Oh yes," she said, "you are exactly who I'm looking for." She gave a harsh laugh. "You don't recognize me, do you?"

I shook my head.

"That's not surprising, I suppose, given what I've been through."

All of a sudden I knew, and I wanted to back away, even shut the door in her face. Elisabeth Avis. The tone of voice identified her.

"Ah," she said, "it's coming back, is it? Well, Miss Harriet, are you going to invite us in?"

"Come in," I said, wishing with all my heart that Sam were there. The air seemed to crackle with anger.

Sam had made me an outdoor oven in which I could bake our bread, once the weather turned mild, without overheating our little house. If he was inordinately fond of sugared tea, he was equally fond of fresh bread, and having no cow, he traded labour for butter at Manor House Farm. I had left the loaves to cool while I went to the shop, and now I felt I had to offer my visitors some bread and butter.

"I would prefer a mug of cold water, if you please. We have walked from the station at Gomshall."

I could see the little man eyeing the bread in a wistful fashion, and so, after bringing the water for Elisabeth, I made the tea, sliced some bread and brought out a crock of preserves. The man was a strange creature. The fingers of his left hand drew inward towards the palm, making his hand resemble a chicken's foot, although his right hand, which clutched a pair of threadbare gloves, looked perfectly normal. I wondered how and where these two had met.

Elisabeth, who had so far refused my invitation to sit, withdrew a book from her carryall and thrust it at me.

"I can only assume you have seen this, seeing as you and he were as thick as thieves."

"I'm sorry, I don't understand." The little man, who had not yet been introduced — I could not help but think of witches and their familiars, although weren't cats the usual companions? — could not keep his eyes away from the table, but he was too cowed or too polite to help himself until the invitation was given.

"This book!" She was practically shrieking. "This dreadful volume, where both of us have been libelled!"

"Please sit down. I confess I don't know what you are talking about."

"I find that hard to believe." She appeared to be coming to a boil, but I had no idea what was upsetting her so. I really wished she would just go away.

"I thought you were in Australia," I said.

"Of course you did, everybody did. Certainly *he* did, or he would never have dared do what he has done."

"He?" I poured out the tea and offered cream and sugar, but she waved me away impatiently. The little man, however, accepted gratefully, poured his tea into his saucer and blew on it to cool it.

"He is Charles Dickens of course. Don't play the innocent with me." She held up the book again and shook it as if she would like to shake it to pieces.

"I am not trying to deceive you," I said. "I honestly don't know what you are going on about. I haven't seen Mr. Dickens for many years."

"You haven't?"

"No, not since I moved back here."

"But you must have read his books? Even in this backwater people must read his books. Why, he has a following of millions."

"I'm afraid I'm not one of those millions. He used to send me a small parcel of books at Christmastime, but that stopped over ten years ago. I must confess I have not kept up. It's mostly children's stories these days, or stories from the Bible."

"Ha," she said with a smile of satisfaction. "Then you really don't know." (The little man was on his third slice of bread and jam.) "That makes it even better. I thought perhaps you didn't mind, you were such a hero-worshipper in the old days. I thought perhaps you had said, 'Use me as you will.' For used you certainly have been, and I, too. Cruelly used."

I began to suspect what had happened.

"He has written about you?"

"Us! About *us*. He has caricatured us, myself most cruelly. At least you get to reform in the end."

She paused at this point, accepted a cup of tea and looked around her. I tried to see my little home the way she must see it, the simple but beautiful furniture Sam had made, the geraniums on the windowsill, the bunches of herbs hanging from the rafters, the braided rug before the fender. Everything neat and tidy, but not much more grand, except for the furniture, than an ordinary tenant-farmer's cottage.

"Somehow I thought you had more ambition than *this*."

"I am quite content with *this*, as you call it, quite content. Can you tell me what it is you want of me, exactly?"

"I want you to join me in a suit against him — against the great man himself. He mustn't get away with this. And we shall be joined by others. I have already found a woman, very small, smaller than Hopkins here, a dwarf, really, who was bought off with a pittance years ago. There must be dozens of us scattered about, and I intend to find them all. Hopkins, show her the advertisement."

Out of a rusty pocket Hopkins produced a folded paper and handed it to me. He had neglected to wipe his fingers, and so he left grease stains and a purple thumb print at the corner. I unfolded it carefully.

"This is to go in all the London newspapers next week," Elisabeth said. "And then the innocent victims will come forth to be counted, and we shall launch such a suit against him, he'll wish he'd never been born. His reputation has already been tarnished, you know. He separated from his wife some years ago, as good as shoved her out the door. He tried to hush it all up, but I've discovered there were plenty of rumours. He's a whited sepulchre, he is, and we shall bring him down."

The advertisement said that anyone who felt they had been held up to ridicule in any of the novels or stories of the noted author Mr. C_____ D_____ should please contact the offices of Messrs. Grundig and Beckstein immediately, with the view of initiating a suit for malicious libel against the said C_____ D_____ and his publishers.

I folded up the paper and handed it back to Hopkins.

"What will you gain by this?"

"Money, of course, but that is not the main thing. All my life I have been subjected to insults and backbiting. All my life I have turned the other cheek, as the Bible instructs us. Well, I am tired of turning the other cheek. I want revenge. He cannot use me like this — it's shameful. I wish I had never seen Urania Cottage!"

"Surely he has not caricatured Urania Cottage?"

"Of course not, he's too clever for that. He wouldn't want to get in trouble with his rich friend. And Urania Cottage is no more, I hear, but that is by the way. No, what I meant is that if I hadn't been persuaded to go there, I would never have met Mr. Dickens and," she added in a low voice, "would never have set foot in Australia."

She stood up, the book on her lap falling to the floor, came over to me and pushed up her sleeves.

"Mark this, Harriet, mark this." There were deep and dreadful scars across both wrists.

"Australia did that," she said, "Australia did that to me. All their fine talk about a new life and a second chance. Well, I can tell you it was far worse than the old life, far worse."

"But the Bishop of Adelaide . . . ?"

She pushed down her sleeves, picked up the book off the floor and resumed her seat.

"The Bishop of Adelaide was another whited sepulchre — he and his wife both. At first it was all smiles and commissions to do altar cloths and stoles and the like, but they had a daughter for whom they had plans. And when the curate of a nearby church began to take a lively interest in me — I did nothing to encourage it — they soon told him of my background, that I had been in prison, and he turned away from me towards their rabbit-toothed daughter. He proposed, was of course accepted, and they had the nerve to ask me to make the wedding kneelers, 'since your work is so very fine, my dear.' Well, of course I refused, and I asked to be transferred somewhere else. I said that I keenly felt their dislike of me and it was making me ill.

"Out of spite or perhaps real cruelty, they sent me away to a horrible rough settlement, where I was supposed to be a housekeeper but was really nothing but a slave to a drunken vicar in a rundown vicarage, nothing but a slave. And I, a clergyman's daughter! The way he ran that parish was a disgrace. There was no one of any culture within a hundred miles, the women — great red-faced, rough things — were as bad as the men, and the children ran wild, like animals. I wrote to the bishop, I begged him to find me another situation, but his wife replied that they were sorry, they had done all they could, then quoted second Thessalonians to me: 'Be not weary in well-doing, for in due season we shall reap if we faint not.'

"And then this, this beast, this disgrace to the cloth had the nerve to ask me to marry him. I couldn't stand it. I stole his razor and slit my wrists."

"Oh my God," I whispered, "you poor woman."

"I wanted to die, but he found me and took me to a hospital, where they locked me up and said I was mad. I was there for a long time until they finally let me go.

"And then I made my way to Sydney and threw myself on the mercy of the nuns there. I told them I wanted to return to England and would work for them, do anything, not just needlework, if they would let me earn passage money. They were good women, but frugal. There was a story you read to us once, about a girl who is assigned some monumental task which seems as though it can never be completed. That's how I felt. And always hungry, always practising 'self-denial.' Except for the Mother Superior and her pets, of course, you could smell the wine on their breath, see the cake crumbs at the corners of their mouths. But I said nothing, just worked away, all for the love of God and the sake of a few shillings a month. Finally, this year, I had enough for the cheapest passage. How happy I was to see the shores of that dreadful country shrink into nothing.

"I kept to myself on the ship. The passengers in my class were mostly ticket-of-leave men and a scattering of missionary wives and children. Few women ever return from that fatal shore. As soon as I arrived in London, I went straight to Urania Cottage to find Mr. Dickens or Miss Burdett-Coutts or someone and demand that they help me. Only Urania Cottage was to let, Miss Burdett-Coutts was out of the country — or so her servants said — and Mr. Dickens was at his new home outside Rochester. I wrote to him at once, but he did not favour me with an answer. However, I have a bit of money left over from my work at the convent, and I have temporarily put up in a respectable lodging house. It was in the landlady's parlour that I found a set of Mr. Dickens's novels, and as I could barely afford a newspaper and my evenings were long and lonely — the landlady, a widow, has a group of friends and invited me to join them in the evenings, but I could tell this was only out of politeness — I began reading.

"He is nothing if not prolific, but I am a quick reader. Last month I finally got to this one" — she banged her fist on the book in her lap — "saw what he had done and became determined to show him up, to reveal him to the world as the fiend he really is. Frankly, if he knows what's good for him he'll offer to settle out of court. We will agree to that, but once we have the money, which will be distributed fairly, according to the degree of insult — remember his old marks system — once we have the money, then we'll publish it to the world and ruin him."

"Can you do that? I know nothing about the law, but surely if you agree to a settlement, you agree to keep quiet. You probably sign something to that effect, perhaps a bond."

"I care nothing for bonds or silences."

I stared at her. (Hopkins had fallen asleep during Elisabeth's tirade; I wondered what was his role in all this.)

"Mr. Dickens is a wealthy man. He will be able to hire the very best lawyers. Do you really think you have a chance?"

"Listen," she said — she was practically spitting — "in the case of this dwarf, Mrs. Hill her name is, she was a neighbour of Mr. Dickens and he caricatured her in *Great Expectations*. Have you read it?

"Yes. I've read up to and including *Bleak House*, which, if you've read it, should put you off lawsuits, I would think."

She ignored this.

"Well, he made Mrs. Hill into Miss Mowcher, do you re-member her?"

"Yes, she's a dwarf. But wasn't she ultimately seen as wise and kind?"

"What difference does that make? Suppose you called attention in public to Hopkins's deformity, ridiculed it, but then went on to say, 'but his left hand is quite beautiful, with long, slender fingers,' do you think you would make Hopkins feel any better? And in my case, he mentions no redeeming features, none. In any event, Mrs. Hill wrote to the man, and then her solicitor wrote and threatened a suit, and Mr. Dickens agreed to change the character when the one-volume edition was pub-lished. That's what you must have read."

I nodded.

"Had I seen this book in its monthly parts, I would have been on to him right away, and I would not have settled for an apology or a promise of minor changes. It's too late for that now, of course, so we shall attack him head on."

How sure she was in her rage. Her eyes glittered; she almost seemed to preen herself, like a bird.

"I still have not read the book," I said, "and so I do not know what he wrote — about either of us. And I'll tell you frankly that I'm not sure I want to read it."

"You must! You must! I am counting on your help. He pretended you were a great favourite of his and he has used you badly."

"How do you know it's me?"

She smiled a horrible smile.

"You may have changed your last name when you were at Urania Cottage, but once I recognized the physical likeness —

and the girl in the novel is very like — then I did a little sleuthing. I went to the Foundling and said I was a long-lost friend just back from Australia. They confirmed that it was you. He calls you 'Tattycoram.'"

"Mother," said Rosie, running in with the dogs at her heels, "who were those queer people walking away from our street? They looked like blackbirds, a rook and a starling." I could not answer her, I was in such distress.

Elisabeth had insisted upon leaving the book with me, and that night, after Rosie was in bed, I regarded it with great misgiving. I felt deeply sorry for Elisabeth, but I did not want anything to do with her, nor, however I might have been caricatured by my former employer, did I want anything to do with this lawsuit. She had left her address and I was supposed to communicate with her as soon as possible. Supposing I just wrapped up the book and sent it back unread. Would she then leave me alone?

Twice I picked up the book, *Little Dorrit* — it was a thick volume of hundreds of pages — and twice I put it down again. I had not promised to read it. I thought of the fat boy who sat in the lodge at the entrance to Doughty Street, how Mr. Dickens had said, "I conjure 'em up in my writing and then they appear in the flesh." The reverse, of course, could be equally true. They appear and then he turns them into fiction. Tattycoram. How could he have used that hated name? How could he?

In the end my curiosity got the better of me; I began to read: "Thirty years ago Marseilles lay burning in the sun, one day." In the second chapter both Elisabeth and I make our appearance.

"It's not you, Hattie," Sam said.

I had just finished reading aloud the last chapter. "Except for the physical description and the use of that name, she's nothing like you."

I smiled at him. "Well of course you would say that, my dear, but the truth is she is like me — or one part of me as I was when I was younger. So that girl is both me and not me. There is a Tattycoram inside, there always has been, one who is fierce and proud, one who would have been capable of great resentment if she'd had to be a maid to somebody like Pet. As it was, I had Miss Georgy to contend with, and I couldn't always dampen down my temper when she was around." I told him about the "costume" for the fancy-dress party and how I threw a teacup against the wall.

"That was when Mr. Dickens advised me to count to two and twenty when my temper was up. He was very good to me. I should have been dismissed and sent back to the Foundling that night. He was always good to me, Sam, and so was she."

"It was not nice to use your real name and your appearance."

"Well, my real name isn't Tattycoram, remember? It's Harriet Coram. But he remembered what the raven said — taught by Miss Georgy, I'm pretty certain — and he saw how deeply I resented it. He is a man who notices such things. It isn't nice, what he's done, but he understands her resentment, and he understands about foundlings and children born out of wedlock. He was a good friend of Mr. Brownlow's and took an interest in the hospital. I do feel used, nevertheless, but I can't seem to get worked up about it."

"The portrait of Miss Wade is quite savage."

"Yes it is, although isn't it strange that he makes her such a handsome woman? Elisabeth was never handsome, although she was a far cry better looking when she lived at Urania Cottage than she is now, poor thing. He has made us both better-looking than we really were."

"Not you, Hattie."

"Yes, me." I sighed. "I can see why she is so angry. He has forced her to look in the mirror, and even though he has changed the circumstances, even though parts of the story are completely made up, that long bit where she relates her history is exactly in her voice. She has always been her own worst enemy."

"Would you sue, if you were in her place?"

"I don't think so, but I don't really know what it feels like to *be* her. Even if she is partly to blame, her life has been one of disappointment and despair. Honestly, I don't think the papers will run her ad, for that advertisement itself might seem to be libellous."

"What will you do?"

"What would you advise me to do? I don't want my name to be added to any petition, yet I feel she will implicate me anyway. I can't very well deny that I was the model for Tattycoram. Nor can he, if she confronts him."

"I think you should send the book back and simply tell her you are not interested in pursuing the matter. Just that. Don't admit to the likeness, don't seem to encourage her in any way, don't wish her good luck."

Our sheep had recently been sheared, and Rosie and I were busy teasing, carding and spinning. Our hands were smooth and soft from handling the fleece. That night I felt such a strong desire to touch my husband, to be assured of his reality in my life, that I offered to massage his back. He never took his shirt off in public, not even on the hottest of summer days, and I was the only one who was intimate with the dreadful raised welts that criss-crossed his body, all the way from his shoulders to his waist and below. As I kneaded his muscles with my softened hands and traced with my fingers the dreadful souvenirs of his life as a convict, I thought of Elisabeth and those self-inflicted scars on her wrists and of her solitude and unhappiness. I remembered Grandfather and how he would touch a person's face with his fingertips, reading the soul within. He would have read Sam's scars and known the history of his suffering, have touched Elisabeth's wrists and absorbed her desperation. All I could do was to rub my husband's back and let him know how much I loved him.

He turned over and smiled at me. "Ah, Hattie, that was grand."

Later, just before I fell asleep, I whispered to him, "Are you still awake?"

"Hmm. What is it?"

"Sam, the Misses Bray are great admirers of Mr. Dickens, as are the schoolmaster and his wife. There may be others nearby, and they must all have read that novel. The Misses Bray at least would recognize me, yet they have never said a word."

"Well there you are then," Sam said, and turned to sleep.

"Sam?" I whispered.

"Hmm?"

"I would never have gone back to those Meagles."

I began to laugh and then he joined in. We laughed until we ran out of breath. Just holding on to one another, laughing.

15

After we sent off the parcel and note, we heard nothing more from Elisabeth Avis. I hoped she had abandoned the idea of bringing a suit against Mr. Dickens, but somehow I didn't think she would. Here was a woman who had seen an insult in every corner all her life; now that she had a genuine grievance, I felt she would never let it go until she had caused real trouble for the perpetrator. Sam hadn't been there during our interview; he had not seen her face nor heard her voice nor felt the heat rise off her like a bonfire. What she couldn't see, so caught up was she in her fury, was that any such suit would only call attention to herself in a most unpleasant way. She — or her solicitor — would have to stand up in court and say she was the "Miss Wade" of the novel and admit to saying similar things to Mr. Dickens when she was at Urania Cottage. And he might even summon Matron and me as witnesses. I felt terribly sorry for her but I did not like her, and I shuddered at the thought of standing up in court with everyone looking at me. Elisabeth would be sure to point out that I was also caricatured in the same novel and would drag in Mrs. Hill and whoever else she'd been able to round up.

"Father," Rosie said one evening, "Mam is brooding."

Sam smiled at me.

"Are you brooding, Hattie?"

"No, no, I am just thinking about a new way to finish off this chain." I held up the double row of tatting I was working on. That satisfied Rosie, who went back to frowning over her lessons, but Sam wasn't fooled. After Rosie had taken herself upstairs, he spoke to me again.

"Is it that woman?"

"Yes." And I told him what I had been thinking. "If I were summoned as a witness for either side, would I have to go?"

"I believe you would."

"I don't think I could bear it. Mr. Dickens is such a famous man the newspapers will print every word."

"He may settle out of court for that very reason."

"I doubt she would let it end there. She as much as told me she wouldn't stop until the public knew how he had betrayed her confidence, how he had used her."

"Well he did, and you as well, and Lord knows who else."

"He probably doesn't see it that way, Sam. I think he's like that raven of his, Grip. Something — or someone — catches his interest, and so he helps himself to a bit, buries it in the back of his mind and digs it up when he wants it. Don't forget, the last time he saw Elisabeth was nearly twenty years ago, the day before she set sail for Australia. He found her troublesome at Urania Cottage — we all did — but I doubt he had any idea then of using her in a story years later. Or using me."

"Do you think what he did was wrong?"

"Probably. But I'm not a genius."

"I think certain rules of behaviour with respect to the personal histories of others apply to geniuses as well as to ordinary folk."

"Yes, *you* think that. But maybe geniuses don't. Maybe such scruples never occur to them." I hesitated. "Sam, when you went out poaching as a lad, did you ever think about getting caught?"

"No. I thought I was far too clever. Oh, it may have been there at the back of my mind, but that just added to the excitement." He grinned. "Are you trying to link me with Mr. Dickens, Hat?"

"It was just a thought."

"It won't work, for if we were caught, we'd have hurt no one but ourselves. As I know to my cost."

I came and stood behind his chair and put my hands on his shoulders. How grey he was getting!

"I shouldn't have brought it up, Sam, I'm sorry."

"No matter, love." He reached up and grabbed my hand. "You are troubled by all this and so you are casting about for answers. Perhaps you are trying to defend him because he was your benefactor. I can understand that. And you have observed him at close quarters; you are in a better position to talk about him than I am. Nevertheless, there is no excuse for bad behaviour of this kind, this careless cruelty, this disregard for the feelings of others. If either side calls you as a witness, the facts will speak against him, not you."

I lay awake all night beside my sleeping husband. Was Elisabeth sleepless too, in her rented bed in Lant Street, or was she sitting up far into the night, writing page after page of indictments against Mr. C_____ D_____?

I was awake to listen to the cocks crow and to hear Rosie tiptoe downstairs to make the tea. How different our lives had turned out, Elisabeth's and mine. I was convinced that part of her history was true: that she had never been loved as a child and that she had sensed this at a very early age. Had I only my experience at the hospital to go on, might not my heart have become bitter and my soul deformed?

Rosie called from the bottom of the stairs, "Mam, Pa, tea is up!" Then she went out to feed the dogs and see to the chickens.

By the afternoon I knew what I wanted to do.

"Are you sure?" Sam said.

"I'm sure. I need to talk to him."

"I'll come with you."

"No, you'll stay here with Rosie. I'll start out early and be home before dark. The days are long just now. I'll take the train from Gomshall to Guildford and change to the Rochester train; I've got it all worked out."

"I don't like you making this journey by yourself."

"I have to do it. This affair is robbing me of my peace of mind. If I can at least talk to him, then whatever happens, I'll feel better."

"Wouldn't a letter do?"

"I thought of that, but no. Even years ago he got masses of letters — many of them begging letters — and no doubt he has a secretary now who sorts his mail. My letter might be put aside, and then if the matter does come to trial and I'm forced to be a witness, he'll never know how troubled I feel."

"What if he won't see you?"

"If he won't, he won't. I can but try."

It was only my second time on a train, and I found it quite amazing how the landscape flew by backwards — villages and trees, fields of grain and coppices, two white horses galloping away from the shrieking monster, small boys waving and disappearing. It had rained in the night, a soft June rain, and now the whole world sparkled. I had the sensation that I was sitting still while the countryside beyond the window unrolled before me like a diorama. We were out of Surrey and into Kent in the blink of an eye. Hopfields and more hopfields, orchards, rolling hills, and then suddenly we were there — the great beast stopped but panting still — carriage doors opening and closing, people rushing away.

It was almost noon, so I walked down the hill and along the High Street, and, the day being fine, I decided to eat my bread and cheese and pickle in the courtyard of the great cathedral, where I saw others enjoying the sunshine. I inquired of an elderly cleric where I might find Mr. Dickens's house, and he replied that Mr. Dickens did not live in Rochester itself, but at Gad's Hill, about eight miles out of the town. I hadn't counted on that, but I was wearing my stout boots, and a good walk sounded just the thing after all that bouncing about on the train. The old man pointed me to a water pump and then to the road that would take me towards Gad's Hill.

"You could have taken the other line," he said, "direct to Higham, and walked through the woods. Next time you'll know."

A part of me wanted to linger — for this was the town in *The Pickwick Papers* — to look inside the cathedral, examine the ruined castle, wander along the streets, but I was not there to sightsee, and I had promised Sam I would be home before it was fully dark. I took the road to Gravesend, as had been suggested by the old man, and reached Higham in under two hours. I stopped to rest and gather my wits and then went on the rest of the way. Gad's Hill was indeed on a hill, opposite the

Sir John Falstaff Inn. The house was set back in extensive grounds and gardens, and, peering through the gate, I noticed his favourite flowers, geraniums, in large stone urns by the front door. There was a sound of hammering and banging around to the side, but I could see no one about, so I walked up the path and knocked at the front door. I heard a dog yapping, but no one came, so I used the knocker once again, with more force. This time footsteps approached along a hall and the door was pulled open. Miss Georgina stood there with a lapdog in her arms.

"Yes," she said, "what is it?"

"I would like to see Mr. Dickens if he is available."

She did not recognize me and I decided not to enlighten her.

"For what reason?"

"For personal reasons, ma'am."

She looked at me, frowned, and shook her head.

"Mr. Dickens cannot be disturbed."

"I could wait."

"He cannot be disturbed. Go away."

And with that she shut the door in my face.

I decided I must try again, this time revealing to her who I was. No doubt she thought I was just a countrywoman wanting to sell him something or ask for money. And so I raised the knocker for a third time. She did not answer, and all I could do was turn away in defeat. Sam was right; I should have written a letter.

The way back to town seemed much longer, and when I finally reached Rochester I was terribly thirsty. I refreshed myself once more at the pump and was debating whether or not to buy a cake to sustain me on the homeward journey and had just crossed the street to look in the baker's window when I saw him in the distance. He was leaning on the fence outside an old brick mansion and had two enormous dogs with him. He seemed so lost in thought that I hesitated to disturb him, but I had not come all this way to leave without speaking to him. I owed him (and owed myself) that courtesy.

The dogs noticed me first; the black one turned his head and growled. "Samson," he said, without looking round, "behave."

"Mr. Dickens," I said quietly, "might I have a word with you, sir?"

At this he turned and smiled, but his eyes were far away. I was shocked by how changed he was; he looked like a man much older than he really was.

"Mr. Dickens," I said, It's me, Hattie. Hattie Coram that was, when you knew me."

He continued to stare at me blankly.

"Tattycoram," I said. "Perhaps you remember Tattycoram?"

What a change came over him then! He started and waved his arms like a windmill, then cried out, in ringing tones, "Woman, I know thee not."

He whistled for his dogs, turned on his heel and rushed away.

By the time I reached Shere, darkness had fallen and Sam and Rosie were out looking for me. It was a fine, still night with a sickle moon, yet my heart was like a stone in my breast.

"Sam," I said, "there was something terribly wrong. For a moment I thought he was going to strike me, and then he ran away before I could talk with him. I was too late. Elisabeth or her solicitor must already have contacted him. He hates me now."

"Come along home, Hattie; we'll have a cup of tea and a bite to eat."

"What is it, Mammy?" said Rosie, taking my basket from me, "What's wrong?"

I told Sam the rest of it after Rosie had gone up to bed.

"I behaved very badly, Sam, I made a scene."

"I reckoned you were keeping something back."

I nodded. "He is still a good walker, but so am I, and I wasn't going to let him deny me like that. I ran after him, calling for him to stop, stop please, just for a moment. He hesitated and I got in front of him just as we passed the inn.

"'Help,' he cried, 'Help me, there is a madwoman here who won't leave me in peace!'

"I was instantly seized and dragged back, away from my old master, who made his escape. I called after him, 'My history was never yours to dispose of, sir, never! I am a real person, sir, not a puppet, a real person!'

"The landlord of the inn held me until a constable arrived. 'Do you know who you were molesting, woman?'

"'Charles Dickens. Yes, I know.'

"'We try to let Mr. Dickens be when he comes into town, try to ignore him, like, as much as possible. And then you cause all this commotion! He is very generous to this town, is Mr. Dickens. Perhaps he won't come again if he knows he is to be disturbed.'

"'I can explain,' I said, and explain I did, but only to say I had been a servant of Mr. Dickens long ago and had come to see him on an important matter.

"'Let go, was you?'

"'No, I was not let go, I had to leave to nurse my mother. Mr. Dickens and I had lost touch, although he was very kind to me — both he and Mrs. Dickens were very kind to me — and I travelled here to warn him . . .'

"'Warn him about what? The landlord here says you was yellin' at him, very angry-like.'

"'Yes. I lost my temper because he wouldn't acknowledge me; I should not have done so; I think he is not a well man.'

"There was some debate among the constable, the landlord and the clientele of the inn as to whether I should be locked up while Mr. Dickens was consulted. In the end they decided to let me go. I asked if I could send a message to Mr. Dickens, stressing that I had come all this way to tell him something important, but the constable, again after consultation, said he thought it was best I go back home and, if I felt it was absolutely necessary, write a letter.

"I was escorted to the station, and the constable stood on the platform until the train actually began to move. I was trembling all over, and I closed my eyes against the curious stares of the other travellers. I did not open them until we arrived at Guild-ford Station."

"I should have gone with you, Hattie."

"No. It was something I had to do on my own. What hurts is that he denied knowing me — and I could see that he *did* know me — and called me a madwoman. I challenged him for something *he* had done, and then he called *me* mad."

"You told me once he did not take kindly to criticism."

"That was true, but when I first addressed him, I wasn't criticizing."

"Your old name was criticism enough. I reckon he thought he'd never see you again."

"And now I still don't know what to do if Elisabeth Avis includes me in her suit."

Two days later the whole world knew that Charles Dickens was dead. Sam bought the London papers so we could read about it. Dead of an apoplexy, they said. Beloved of millions. "Only one year older than myself," Sam said. "They say he wore himself out."

And then, later, an envelope containing an item torn out of a newspaper. "On Friday last, the body of a female was fished out of the Thames below Waterloo Bridge. It has been identified as that of Miss Elisabeth Avis, a recent arrival from Australia and a lodger at number 40, Lant Street. The coroner ruled it a suicide, and from certain marks on the body it was clear that suicide had been attempted at least once before."

Poor woman. Poor woman. Hopkins, whoever he was, must have had the grim task of identifying her. There was no accompanying note, just the article.

"Well," Sam said, "she won't bother anyone again, poor soul."

Mr. Dickens was buried in Westminster Abbey. The papers said thousands of people, rich and poor, lined up to pay their respects. For thirty-three years, in one way or another, my life had been entangled with his. In spite of his recent bizarre behaviour, I could not judge him harshly and was sorry he was gone.

At sunset we walked onto the Downs — Sam, myself, Rosie and the two dogs — and looked out over the beloved hills. Midsummer's Eve was fast approaching, and the land lay before us as still as a landscape in a painting, while the sky changed from deep pink to streaks of orange, and the bright ball of the sun sank lower and lower until it disappeared altogether. We spoke not a word to one another, just drank in the beauty of the scene, absorbed it, witnessed the going down of the sun, sure in our hearts that it would rise again the next morning.

A nightingale sang, far away, and I thought to myself, how could I be any happier than I am at this moment? I have been one of the lucky ones.

"Mam's crying," Rosie said, touching my cheek. "Why are you crying, Mam?"

If this were one of Mr. Dickens's novels, I might feel obligated to go on and tie up everything neatly, complete my history and the history of my family. But this is real life and I have no idea what the future holds. I could predict that Sam and I will grow old together, stiff in the joints like Digger and Angus, shortsighted, perhaps a little querulous and cranky. The real future lies with Rosie. Will she stay in the village or go? She says she wants to be a teacher, or perhaps a nurse, like Miss Nightingale. There is a certain restlessness in her — I notice it more and more — which may lead her to seek out a livelier place than this. I watch her running barefoot down the lanes or across the fields, her red hair gleaming like a bright beacon of hope.

Someday soon I will take her up to London, take her to Guildford Street. We'll stand outside the hospital gates and I'll tell her my story. Sam says she probably knows most of it — our village is too small — but she has never asked a single question, which is unlike her. Perhaps she is waiting for us to begin. Someday soon, but not just yet, not just yet. Never again will she be as free as she is now.

Sometimes, when I am in a melancholy mood, I think about the woman who gave birth to me and about women like her, and I have an awful vision: a multitude of women, hurrying through the streets of London, coming from Southwark, Cheapside, Camden Town, Wapping, from wherever women live, that is to say, from everywhere, all in black shawls, each carrying within her shawl the living proof of her shame. Hundreds of them, thousands (nearly fifty years ago, was I not No. 19,176, Girl?).

Platoons, companies, battalions, regiments of women. And in my vision the salt of their tears creates a vast inland sea, upon which float millions of little candles in memory of the children they have given up. And I see my mother amongst them, with curly black hair, as black as a raven's wing, clutching me to her breast for the last time.

All the Rachels, weeping for their children.

And the line stretches out, the hordes of women keep coming. Will it never stop?

Acknowledgements

I would like to thank the following libraries, museums, individuals and funding bodies for their help and support during the writing of this novel: the staff at the British Library; the staff at the London Metropolitan Archives; Mr. Don Staples, volunteer librarian at the Dickens Museum, Doughty Street, London; Rhian Harris at the Foundling Museum, Brunswick Square, London; the museum at Shere; Valerie Glassman and Ruth Slavin, for additional research in London; Marybeth Hovenden, of Guildford, Surrey; Kate Dallyn, of Foxton, Albury, Surrey; the British Columbia Arts Council; and the Canada Council for the Arts.

And, as always, my cheerful typist, Carole Robertson.